"Such A Delicate Face," Came His Half Whisper.

"So fragile. Do you know what a delicate face you have? Makes a man want to go slay a dragon or two...or at least an alligator." The humor left his eyes, replaced by an odd intensity. His thumb moved down her neck and back again. "Soft skin, so warm and smooth. Like satin..."

"CC, don't," Valerie warned.

"What is the matter?" CC asked, though he knew full well what the problem was—this minor bit of loveplay was arousing explosive feelings. He wanted her, right here, he didn't care where, just as long as they were together.

Valerie pulled away, trying to conceal the pulse beating wildly at the base of her throat. "CC, I'd like to kiss you. But I'm not ready to go beyond that."

Something shadowed her eyes, something that gentled his heart. "I think you are. But I'll try to restrain myself, Valerie."

Dear Reader,

When I think of autumn, I think of cool, crisp November nights curled up by the fire . . . reading a red-hot Silhouette Desire novel. Now, I know not all of you live in cooler climes, but I'm sure you, too, can conjure up visions of long, cozy nights with the hero of your dreams.

Speaking of heroes, Dixie Browning has created a wonderful one in MacCasky Ford, the hero of her *Man of the Month* book, *Not a Marrying Man*. Mac is a man you'll never forget, and he certainly meets his match in Banner Keaton.

November is also a time of homecoming, and Leslie Davis Guccione has been "away from home" for far too long. I know everyone will be glad to see her back with *A Gallant Gentleman*. And if you're looking for something tender, provocative and inspirational, don't miss Ashley Summer's *Heart's Ease*. This story is one I feel very strongly about, and I'd be interested in hearing how you like it.

Rounding out November are a delicious love story from Raye Morgan, *Baby Aboard,* a fiery romp by Carole Buck, *Red-Hot Satin,* and a sexy, spritely tale by Karen Leabo, *Lindy and the Law.*

So, until next month, happy reading!

Lucia Macro
Senior Editor

ASHLEY SUMMERS

HEART'S EASE

SILHOUETTE *Desire*®

Published by Silhouette Books New York

America's Publisher of Contemporary Romance

SILHOUETTE BOOKS
300 East 42nd St., New York, N.Y. 10017

HEART'S EASE

ISBN: 0-373-05675-3

First Silhouette Books printing November 1991

Printed in the U.S.A.

Books by Ashley Summers

Silhouette Desire

Fires of Memory #36
The Marrying Kind #95
Juliet #291
Heart's Delight #374
Eternally Eve #509
Heart's Ease #675

Silhouette Romance

Season of Enchantment #197
A Private Eden #223

ASHLEY SUMMERS

is an incurable romantic who lives in Texas, in a house that overflows with family and friends. Her busy life revolves around the man she married thirty years ago, her three children and her handsome grandson, Eric. Formerly the owner and operator of a landscaping firm, she also enjoys biking, aerobics, reading and traveling.

To Doreen Walsh, with love and admiration

One

Decisions, Valerie Hepburn thought as she stepped from the shower. Always decisions. It wasn't that she didn't like making decisions, but she had so much to lose if she made the wrong one. Taking up the towel she'd laid out beforehand, she wiped at the water streaming down her alabaster shoulders to the perfection of one rose-tipped breast...and the empty plane beside it. The small, curving globe looked so vulnerable in its aloneness that she felt an ache clamp her midriff.

Hurriedly she averted her glance and continued her brooding reflections. Decisions, she thought again with a hard sigh. And changes. Radical changes, some of them, capable of destroying all inner sunlight. Or at the least, of altering her entire way of life. Could she stand yet another?

"Well, of course you can *stand* it—you're a survivor, aren't you?" she scolded her grave-faced image. But did she *want* another change in what had finally become a stabilized life-style? She'd been here four days now, visiting with her sister and mulling over the possibility of leaving her home in Clinton, Mississippi, for this charming little Texan town just forty minutes away from a huge, bustling city. But there was so much to consider. Mainly her children, she acknowledged, and how they would react.

Irritably she shrugged. There was no telling what they would say to a move, so why fret it? she demanded of her worrywart self. She'd know how they'd react when she told them—*if* she had anything to tell them.

Dropping that unrewarding bit of speculation, she swirled the towel down her back. Across the room, a white Persian cat named Dempsey—he'd fought every cat in the neighborhood and won—yawned and stretched luxuriously. Stephanie's cat, she thought, her smile tender. During these past few days she had gotten reacquainted with her sister— her half sister, she amended, for they'd had different fathers—and been caught up in Stephanie's busy social circle.

"Maybe a little too caught up," Valerie murmured, noting the faint shadows beneath her eyes. But having any social life at all was fascinating in itself. Especially a safe one.

Safe was the key word, she admitted wryly. She was one month short of forty and petrified by even the thought of dating.

Bending over, her russet hair falling across her face like a curtain, she began drying her long legs. If she was dead set on worrying, Valerie admonished herself, then she'd do well to remember that she was also investing her late husband's insurance money in the plant–nursery she and Stephanie had inherited from an aunt. It was a daring thing to do, and she wondered what he would have thought had he but known. Although he had been a wonderful mate, Robert wasn't a man to take risks.

But she trusted her sister. Stephanie was one sharp lady when it came to business. Three years ago the nursery had been a small mom-and-pop affair. It would have remained so had not she decided otherwise. In order to expand their business she had mortgaged this house, left to her by the same aunt. When that proved inadequate, she had managed to obtain another loan to buy an adjoining parcel of land for further expansion.

It was freeway frontage and an expensive venture, yet Valerie had readily agreed to the debt. As an accountant, she knew how to read balance-sheet projections. Purchasing the frontage had been a financially sound move. But they still needed costly landscaping equipment and, after months of agonizing, she had liquidated her modest portfolio and put the proceeds into their jointly owned company.

"You won't be sorry, I promise you," Stephanie had vowed.

Valerie hoped not. She had two children to put through college.

"Hey, Val, you home?" A lilting female voice shattered her reverie. An instant later, a vibrant strawberry blonde exploded through the bedroom's open door.

Valerie froze, feeling nakedly exposed. Unaware of time's passing, she had left the bathroom door ajar, and Stephanie slipped on through, saying gaily, "Oh, there you are! Listen, I hope you've fixed something fabulous for supper tonight because—"

She stopped short, looking stricken as Valerie shot erect and jerked the bath towel to her chest. Pink terry cloth tumbled down to cover her from collarbone to thighs, but she still resembled a stone-carved statue.

Stephanie flung out her hands, palms up. "Oh, Val, I'm sorry, I—I didn't think you'd mind me coming on in!"

Valerie's stiff, rejecting stance slowly relaxed as she responded to her sister's distress. "It's all right, Steffie, I know you didn't mean to offend."

Stephanie's face clouded with hurt. "But you are offended."

Valerie managed a smile, knowing that the younger woman was much more casual than she was about nudity. "Well, a little. I'm just not used to this sort of togetherness," she explained with a wintry hint of wryness.

Relaxing a bit, Stephanie leaned against the marble counter. She spoke softly. "Me, either, actually, but I just...wasn't thinking, I guess. I'll leave if you want... although I would like to see what a mastectomy looks like. For real, I mean, not in some picture. But to see with love, not idle curiosity," she added quickly.

Valerie had tensed at the request, resentful of it. But after a prickly moment of silence, her mouth curved in pained confession. What she resented was more than just an intrusive request. Stephanie was twenty-five, with smooth, creamy skin and a figure that was a symphony of matching curves.

Even that gorgeous red-gold mass of hair was natural. None of which helps, Valerie thought like a jab of self-reproach. When she spoke, her voice emerged low and slightly scratchy.

"It's a difficult thing you're asking of me, Stephanie. I've never shown anyone my...deformity." Elaborately casual, she let the towel fall to her waist. "Not very pretty, is it," she murmured, her gaze alert to any kind of reaction.

Darkening green eyes touched upon the pale pink scar that slanted downward across the flat expanse of skin. "It's not ugly, either," came Stephanie's fierce response. "Honorable battle scars are never ugly."

But her voice broke, and Valerie saw the shock that flashed across her sister's lovely face. Unable to think of an appropriate response to this sweet reassurance, she merely smiled.

"Honest, Val, it's not nearly as bad as I thought it would be," Stephanie persisted. "Thank you for showing me."

She looked up, her gaze too shiny. "Oh, Valerie, my heart breaks when I think of all you've endured. I feel like I've failed you—I should have been there with you—"

"Oh, nonsense, how could you be there with me when *I* didn't even tell you?" Valerie reasoned with an instinctive desire to assuage hurt.

A shake of golden head denied her logic. "I knew about it. Through Aunt Lillian. I just . . . let it lay there, I guess. I can't begin to tell you how sorry I am about that. But you should have told me, Val."

Valerie didn't reply; they'd already been through this.

Sighing, Stephanie went on. "But we weren't really ever that close, were we? That's another reason for you to move here. Not only are we business partners but we're family. My only family since Dad passed on. We should be close, and why not? That fourteen-year gap between our ages isn't that wide anymore. And I think we need each other. I know I need you, anyway," she confessed with touching candor.

"Stephanie, honey, I hear what you're saying. But this is really quite a big decision. And it's my big decision. Don't push, hmm?"

A flicker of a dimple in Stephanie's right cheek betrayed her frustration. "Sorry, I didn't mean to push." She paused, her gaze straying downward, then blurted, "Val, why didn't you seek reconstruction of your breast?"

"It didn't seem important at the time," Valerie said dismissively. Turning to the closet, she drew a deep breath before taking down worn jeans and a big shirt. Talking with Stephanie like this was unsettling. They were both aware that she held the younger woman at arm's length.

Shoulders hunched, she dropped the towel to her waist again and put on her shirt. The moment with Stephanie had been so awkward, she thought sadly. Small wonder she shuddered at the thought of ever baring herself to a man.

"You're not wearing your magic bra?" Stephanie asked with valiant lightness.

"No, not when it's just you and me."

"But it's not just you and me—we're having a dinner guest."

"Oh, Stephanie!" Valerie groaned, half laughing. "This is only my third day here and already you've dragged home two other reluctant bachelors. I told you I'm too old to be fixed up."

"You're not old," Stephanie said impatiently. "Besides, this one is different—"

"He's not an eligible bachelor, then?"

"No. He's a widower. Well, actually, yes, he is, one of the most eligible bachelors in Houston, in fact. I expect he can just about have his pick of beautiful women. But he's not here in that capacity, Val. Besides being a family friend, he's one of our most important clients. C. C. Wyatt, remember? I told you about him."

"Awkwardly, as I recall," Valerie remarked.

"That's because I didn't want you to get the wrong impression. Other people do, especially out on job sites, but they don't matter. You do. My relationship with C.C. is strictly platonic. Well, I'd better get back to the den before he starts thinking he's been totally abandoned. But that outfit, Val..."

Valerie's dark eyes twinkled. "I'll dress appropriately, Stephanie. Now scoot, and shut the door, please? I'll be out to meet your Mr. Wyatt in just a few minutes."

Despite her inherent shyness, Valerie spoke easily. He couldn't be any worse company than those other two overstuffed males Stephanie had brought home.

Besides, it didn't really matter what this C. C. Wyatt person was like, she reflected somewhat smugly. Her indifference to men was a marvelous security blanket.

She rehung the jeans and shirt a little regretfully. Dressing up wasn't one of her favorite things to do. But an important client warranted it.

Skillfully she styled her russet-brown hair in a soft chignon. Pearl-and-sapphire earrings studded her small ears. Grimacing, for she disliked wearing it, she fitted herself into the prosthetic bra, then drew on a satin chemise and tap pants.

A tailored white silk blouse and navy harem slacks, combined with white hose and slippers, completed her costume. With her dark brows and lashes and luminous skin, she had no need for makeup other than a rosy lip gloss. After a brief check in the mirror, she left the room.

A burst of masculine laughter arrested her progress for an instant. The sound pleased something deep inside her.

That laughter also annoyed her. She strode on. Stephanie and her guest had left the den for the solarium, a glassed-in porch filled with plants and wicker furniture. Valerie loved the light-filled room. Her own home was dim and heavily draped. But Robert had liked it that way...

Shaking off the untimely spate of memories, she stepped through the open door and stopped with a silent, indrawn breath. Her pause was so brief as to be imperceptible. But during that split second of time a kaleidoscope of images and thoughts splintered in her mind.

C. C. Wyatt was not another burly male with a belly hanging over his belt. He was tall and broad shouldered, almost rangy in his gray linen shirt and darker gray trousers. A narrow tan belt encircled his trim waist, and a gold watch banded his wrist.

The watch was deceptive. It looked plain, but Valerie had lived in Europe too long not to recognize its quality. On the arm of his chair lay a fawn-colored sports jacket. Cashmere, she noted. His clothes, for all their simplicity, bespoke confident good taste as well as expert tailoring. All plus points, of course, she mocked herself, piqued at such marked attention to detail.

Apparently he was preparing to leave, for he was placing a handsome Stetson hat on his head. Beneath the cream-colored felt, dark gold hair, streaked by summer sun and elegantly frosted with platinum at his temples, gleamed in October's mellow light. A lock fell over his high brow, softening his rugged profile and drawing the gaze downward.

He had a wonderful mustache, darkly gold and dashing. He wore boots, she noted with a pleased little smile. Boots were in character with the image rapidly building in her mind's eye.

The small sound she made brought her face-to-face with him. Intense blue eyes squinted at her through a thicket of dusky lashes. Her gaze glanced off his to encounter delightfully lean, angular features.

As from a great distance, she heard Stephanie moving about in the kitchen. We're alone, she thought distractedly. I don't want to be alone with this man.

"Uh, hello?" she said, a tentative greeting.

He grinned, and those sky-blue eyes crinkled. Lowering his hat, he inclined his head. "Hello."

His voice was incredibly deep, almost gravelly, a vibrato of sound that seemed to dance along her skin. Disconcerted by her awareness of him as a man, she put one foot in front of the other until she reached the hand he stretched out.

"I'm Valerie Hepburn," she said crisply. "Stephanie's sister," she plowed on as his big hand enveloped hers in a remarkably gentle clasp.

"I sort of suspected you were. Pleased to meet you, ma'am," he drawled with a teasing note softening his voice. "I'm C. C. Wyatt."

"My pleasure, Mr. Wyatt."

"C.C."

"C.C.," she echoed. What did "C.C." stand for? Carl? Curtis? Conrad? "Were you leaving?" she asked, glancing at his hat.

"Yeah, I was giving some thought to sneaking out," he admitted sheepishly.

"Why on earth would you do that, Mr. Wyatt?" She liked his name. "C.C.," she amended quickly. Clyde? Chester? Clayton?

"Steph'nie let slip that you weren't keen on company tonight. Not that I blame you—people just dropping in for dinner can be a nuisance, especially if you're not used to it. She went to check on the roast, so I thought, given the opportunity..." He let it trail into a shrug.

"I'm *getting* used to it, or at least to Stephanie's idea of hospitality! It's quite charming, really, and I've cooked more than was needed. Habit, I suppose—unexpected dinner guests were actually common around our family table," Valerie replied with a nervous little laugh she instantly derided. He had removed his hat, this new and unruly part of herself was quick to notice, and his hair, although cut above his collar, was wonderfully thick and springy. She wondered how it would feel to the touch.

Belatedly she withdrew her hand from his and waved toward the chair he had vacated. "Please, sit back down and finish your beer."

Just then Stephanie came rushing back. "Dinner's doing fine, so you sit, too," she admonished her sister. "Here, your favorite wine. You two have met, I see," she observed brightly. "Good, because it's your turn to play hostess while I freshen up."

"I swear, that woman's a regular whirlwind." C.C. sighed as she left the room in a swirl of skirts and flashing limbs.

The fond tolerance in his remark warmed Valerie's heart. "She is that," she agreed mildly. With sinuous grace, she sat down on the hibiscus-patterned couch and crossed her legs. "Young and impulsive, but reliable, too. You can depend on that. She's told me about the business you've thrown her way. Our way, I should say, since I'm her partner. Silent partner, so far. Because I know I can depend on her, too, just as you can."

He had cocked his head. Valerie wondered if she was chattering. There was a scratch on his left hand. She wondered if he'd put something on it.

"Sorry, I didn't mean to run on like that," she said, wrinkling her nose. "What I meant to do, I suppose, was reassure you. Have you put anything on that scratch? It looks swollen."

He looked surprised.

"Sorry again," she murmured. "Force of habit. I'm a mother."

He laughed. "Steph'nie told me you have two kids. Two girls, she said," he replied invitingly.

She chuckled, liking the way he pronounced Stephanie's name. "Yes, twins, Bonnie and Brenda, two giggly ten-year-olds."

"Identical twins?"

"No. They're night and day. Bonnie's true to her name, which means a little, pink angellike creature. She's my sweet, golden child. 'Brenda' means little dark-haired beauty who delights everyone, which she does," Valerie replied, enjoying his interest. "She's also my little tomboy, which causes problems now and then. Wouldn't you like me to put something on that hand? I have some salve in the bathroom that's very good."

"If you think it needs something on it, then we'll put something on it," C.C. decided gravely.

Color flushed her ivory cheeks. She came to her feet with the same beguiling feminine grace and left the solarium.

Odd how the sunlight went with her, C. C. Wyatt thought.

A moment later she was back, salve in hand. In the soft lilac dusk shadowing the fragrant room, she seemed wonderfully tall. He was well over six feet himself, so he appreciated height in a woman.

She was also exquisitely fashioned. Bemusedly C.C. watched her fluid movements. He'd heard of "sylphlike" figures before, but he'd never seen anyone with one. But those narrow shoulders, the gentle swell of breasts and hips, the nipped-in waist and long, sleek thighs outlined by her thin slacks, all flowed together to fit his somewhat fuzzy picture of the word.

His gaze slid upward to her long neck. A swan's neck, he thought, frowning at the poetic descriptions that kept coming to mind. Her big, dark eyes were set wide apart. Vulnerable eyes, at least to him. Doe eyes.

She wasn't beautiful; her mouth was too sweetly generous for her small, precise nose. But she only had the most arresting face he'd ever seen. And the classiest, too, with those sculpted cheekbones, the winged brows, that delicate jut of chin...

He had remained standing. "Please, sit down," she repeated.

Dumbly he obeyed. Strange, but he felt a bit addled.

She snapped on a light and sat down beside him. She smelled better than the room did, he thought. She opened the salve and began stroking it on his scratched hand. Her long, slim fingers were slippery cool on his skin. Startled by his reaction to her light touch, he spoke harshly.

"What you said about me throwing business to Steph'nie, that's not favoritism or anything nasty like that. It's no secret I've got a soft spot in my heart where she's concerned. After all, I've known her since she was a kid. But business is business. You can't build up a reputation for quality work by tolerating incompetence. I gave her a chance, true, but from then on she's had to meet my standards, as well as compete with other firms."

Her lashes swept up. "I didn't mean to imply favoritism, I was merely thanking you for giving her that chance. Certainly we expect nothing more than that, from you or anyone else."

"And *I* didn't mean to ruffle your feathers," he returned gruffly. "I just felt it needed saying. Truth to tell, I've always expected a bit more of her than I did the others, and she's given it. But even my own son would have been sacked had he not been qualified for the job... had he worked for me, which he hasn't. And probably never will."

Valerie didn't miss the twisted smile that accompanied his humorous prediction. Recapping the salve, she wiped her fingers.

"You have a son?"

"You might say that." He averted his eyes. "He's thirty-two, lives in California. We don't have much to do with each other. And probably never will, if he has the say-so about it," he ended on that same, faintly bleak twist of humor.

A sensitive woman, Valerie contained her curiosity. "What's his name?"

"Jordan."

"That's unusual. I'll have to look it up and see what it means." She opened an adhesive bandage and covered his small wound. "I did a paper in college on names and how their meanings relate to real-life character traits."

"And how was that?" C.C. asked, watching with mingled feelings as she released his hand.

"Surprisingly enough, an impressive percentage of names and traits matched." She laughed, a full-throated sound. "I'll look up yours, too, if you tell me what—"

"Randy's here and dinner's ready!" Stephanie interrupted. "I called him a few minutes ago and he came right on over. Chowhound," she teased the handsome male who appeared behind her.

Valerie greeted him warily. She'd met him twice already and thought him nice enough.

C.C.'s greeting was cordial, but she thought she detected a little coolness there. Maybe she'd imagined it, she decided later. Certainly there was no sign of animosity at dinner, which was spiced by lively conversation and laughter.

The meal she had prepared, a boneless, herb-and-spinach stuffed pork roast flanked by shredded potato cakes, disappeared quickly. "You're a very good cook," C.C. said, pleasing her inordinately much, as did the creases his smile carved around his mouth and eyes.

"Thank you. I do love to cook, and it's a delight to prepare something besides corn-chip pie and tuna casserole," she replied dryly.

Dessert was a creamy vanilla-bean mousse served with rose wine in thin, crystalline balloon glasses. C.C. seemed faintly preoccupied, though he did hand her another compliment as if it were a bouquet of flowers. Soon after they'd cleared the table, he thanked them for feeding him and took his leave.

Valerie was relieved to see him go. Being pleased so often and so much in one evening would make any sane woman nervous, she thought irritably.

Soon afterward, Stephanie and her young man headed for a disco. Valerie didn't mind being left alone. She had things to think about. Like the tear in her security blanket.

Thank heavens it was easily mended, she thought as she took down her hair and shook it out. C. C. Wyatt was a very disturbing man.

She slid into bed and drew up the comforter with a yawning sigh. Lord, but she was sleepy. Too sleepy to remember, reflect or want.

But she would like to know what "C.C." stood for. Cliff? Clarence? Charlie...?

Two

With the precision of an alarm clock, Valerie awoke just as first dawn touched her windows. The heady aroma of coffee, set last night to brew at this early hour, wafted up the stairs to entice her from her cozy nest. Barefoot, looking ridiculously young and innocent in white cotton pajamas, she spared only a glance for her mirrored image before hurrying to the kitchen.

She stirred up some blueberry muffins, her favorite breakfast, and put them in the oven. After that she fed the cat. Then, coffee cup in hand, she stepped outside to greet the morning.

It had become a ritual with her, acknowledgment, she supposed, that she was still alive and well. Certainly her dance with death had made her more aware of life.

Perhaps that was why she'd been so alert to every detail that made up the man she had met last night, Valerie mused. Then again, perhaps not. There was no getting around his masculine charms. Confident, a delicious bit macho, attractive and intelligent. Sensitive, too, she suspected. And humorous. The latter was very important in a man.

Not that she was looking for a man, Valerie hastened to assure herself. She'd already had her one and only.

Nor was she in need of a man, she admitted with mixed emotions. It was as if her sexuality had been anesthetized by the devastating surgery she'd been forced to endure. Nothing stirred the strong sensuality she'd once possessed. *Nothing,* she repeated to herself a little defiantly. It was better that way.

Leaving the pink-and-gold dawn, she went to the solarium and curled up on a chaise longue. Dempsey the cat came in and leaped onto her lap. Very soon the fragrance of blueberry muffins joined the toasty smell of coffee hovering in the air. Wrapped in the familiar scents of morning, Valerie closed her eyes and let herself drift into the welcoming warmth of memories.

She had loved her husband, loved being his wife and the mother of his children. They'd met in Europe. She had been young, but the timing was right when they wed. It had been a happy marriage, without doubts or secret longings to mar their splendid joy. He'd been ten years older, established in his career, with money enough for the luxuries she so enjoyed, like a rented villa in the French countryside, shopping in Parisian fashion houses, family outings to ancient castles and picnics made up by Harrods of London. They'd spent every cent that came their way....

Stephanie interrupted her poignant slide into the past with a chiding, "The buzzer was buzzing its head off. Luckily I heard it in time to save the muffins. Here," she said, holding out a napkin-lined basket. "Have one. Oh, Val, it's so good to have you here!"

"It's good to be here, honey," Valerie replied with heartfelt warmth. The younger woman was wearing a shawl-

collared terry-cloth robe. Her golden hair streamed around
its snowy shoulders and wisped about her sleep-flushed face.
So beautiful, Valerie thought, feeling a sudden urge to hug
her sister. "What's on the agenda this morning?" she asked
instead.

"C.C.'s going to meet us at his business complex—the
one on Cypress Way, remember? Did I mention that job?"

Valerie laughed to counter the sudden thrill of excitement in her blood. "I think so, but we've talked so much
I'm having trouble keeping everything in my head. What
time?"

"Ten o'clock. And when C.C. says ten, he means ten
sharp. The man can't abide tardiness."

"Neither can I," Valerie murmured, and Stephanie
blushed. It was a monumental effort to get herself any-
where on time.

"What do you think of C.C.?" she asked. "Gorgeous,
isn't he?"

"Titillating," Valerie conceded. She took another muf-
fin. "What does 'C.C.' stand for?"

"Gee, I don't know. He signs all his papers 'C. C. Wyatt,'
so I have no idea. Why?"

Valerie carelessly lifted a shoulder. "Just curious."

The beauty of dawn struck C. C. Wyatt as an extrava-
gance. He had awakened in a curious mood, neither good
nor bad, but somewhere in between. He'd dreamed of the
past, bits and pieces strewn like confetti through his night.
He'd dreamed of joy and tiny slices of happiness pressed like
wildflowers in a book. But the dreams had been fuzzy edged
this time, fading into formless blurs even while he tried to
hold them.

His expression grew troubled as he picked up the silver-
framed photograph of his only surviving son. Jordan. Ah,
the unforgiving pride of the young, he thought achingly. So

certain they're right, so proudly unneedful. *Jordan, I'm sorry!* It was a cry torn from the heart.

Setting down the picture, he pulled off the towel enwrapping his hips and tossed it into the hamper. Unbidden, thoughts of the woman he had met last night slipped into his mind. An exciting woman, one who kept capturing his gaze regardless of where his attention had been directed. Her hair had gleamed in the soft lamplight. She had wonderful skin, satiny textured and with an indescribable color somewhere between pink and cream and sun-kissed gold. He could still hear her low, rich, throaty laugh, still recall, with a tiny inward shiver, the feel of her slim fingers on his own skin.

It was stimulating to know that he would see her again. He had enjoyed the evening.

And he had hated leaving behind all that warmth and laughter to come home to an empty house.

Then, as now, sadness clawed at him, the talons of a nameless emptiness that had been part of him since his wife's death. Not loneliness, though God knew he was lonely. But that was superficial in comparison. Loneliness could be assuaged, temporarily, anyway. What he felt was so deep and elemental that nothing could touch it or give him heart's ease.

His wife's name had been Hope. A beautiful woman, both inside and out. Tender, warm, caring, laughing. Always laughing. A freeway accident three years ago had torn her and his other, younger son from his life.

He had gone raging into a long darkness, choked with grief and anguish, a torment unlike anything he'd ever known. But eventually he had accepted their deaths, helped along by grueling hours of work that left him too spent to do anything but tumble, exhausted, into sleep. Ironically, in doing so, he had become a very successful man.

So now he was an "eligible, much-sought-after bachelor," free as a bird. Women falling in front of him like rose petals.

Big deal.

Face it, Wyatt, he thought, slashing a brush through his damp hair. You're a family man without a family.

It wasn't quite that simple, of course. Life never was, he reflected with a sardonic twist of mouth.

His first marriage had been a manipulative tactic used to give his son a name.

His second had been a glory and a wonder to him.

But its loss had torn the guts right out of his life, and he couldn't face that again.

The way to avoid that *was* simple, appallingly so. He would neither fall in love nor marry again.

Pouring himself another cup of coffee from the service beside his bed, he wondered if Valerie Hepburn liked impromptu picnics.

Valerie and Stephanie arrived at the job site five minutes early, driving down a double-laned entrance divided by an esplanade planted with flame-red crepe myrtles and low-growing, dark green junipers. The blossoms of the small, treelike myrtles really did resemble crepe paper, Valerie thought.

"Beautiful," she said.

"Well, of course!" Stephanie lilted. "C.C. thought so, too, thank goodness," she added, leading Valerie to wonder if she was really so cocky after all.

They parked in front of a wide, four-story building constructed of opaque blue glass and white stone. Apparently it was to be a medical facility, for there was an aluminum doctor's symbol by the front entrance.

Valerie listened as her sister related the completed landscaping plan. But her real interest was held by the building itself. It looked like C.C., she thought, all clean, spare lines and tempered strength. With a self-chiding smile, she brought her attention back to the matter at hand.

"After the shrubs are in," Stephanie was saying, "We'll lay flats of grass, water it in and voilà! No more new, raw look. I hope we can finish this today because we've got another, similar job beginning the first of the week. And with only one crew... But that's due to change, too, just as soon as your money becomes working capital."

She looked at Valerie, her eyes brilliant. "Val, don't you worry, we'll make this business a success, you'll see. With clients like C.C. and the Etharton Group—that job we're starting Monday—we can't miss as long as we fulfill our part of the bargain. And we will, I'll see to that."

Valerie murmured something soothing. Her attention had wandered again, snagged this time by the man getting out of a sleek navy pickup truck.

Her heart thudded wildly. Valerie couldn't have looked away even if she had wanted to. Which she didn't, for looking at C. C. Wyatt was pure, feminine pleasure.

His lithe torso was clad in a blue chambray shirt with sleeves rolled to his elbows, exposing strong, bronzed arms sprinkled with golden brown hair. Lean, faded jeans encased his muscular thighs and long legs. A battered gray Stetson sat on his gilded head in counterpoint to the scuffed black boots he wore.

She wondered how his mustache would feel against her skin.

Her already heightened senses flared to embrace the nearness of him as he stopped beside her and took off his hat.

"Good morning" was all he said, but he said it in a voice so rich and deep her skin tingled as if from a caress.

"Good morning," she returned. She couldn't help the coolness in her voice. He disconcerted her.

Stephanie, too, wished him a good-morning, then they settled down to business. Valerie listened, trying to take it all in.

But she was too distracted. He still wore her bandage on his hand, and she remembered the feel of his skin under her fingers. He smelled spicy, like a sandalwood forest after a rain, she thought.

The timbre of his voice, although still a rich bass sound, had a certain brusqueness to it when talking business, she discovered. Intuitively she knew that he would be slow to anger, but that it would burn deep.

She also knew that he would be a passionate lover.

Startled at her mental wanderings, she warned herself to stick to business. He was sweet, seductive danger walking around on two feet, and she had enough to deal with already.

He glanced at her. "Well, what do you think, Valerie? Does this meet your high standards?" he asked teasingly.

As he waved a hand encompassing the handsome building and its backdrop of tall pines, a gold signet ring flashed in the sunlight. He wore it on his ring finger. As compensation for the wedding band it had once borne? She knew the feeling. She, too, wore a heavy ring on her third finger to offset the insecurity caused by her loss.

A sense of weakness gripped her as his gaze swept down her sweater and skirt. It was late October, yet the day was hot and humid. Not a breeze stirred. She was suddenly starkly aware of the white cotton fabric clinging to her upper body, molding her pert breast and its custom-made counterpart.

She could never expose her body to a man like C. C. Wyatt.

Startled, she quickly brushed the errant thought aside. "It's a very nice building C.C., I like it."

He cocked his head to one side as he looked down at her. There was a crookedness to his smile that angled his mustache beguilingly. Her fingertips burned to trace the just-visible outline of his upper lip. Every part of him made an impact on her senses that surprised and alarmed when it wasn't stroking soft, responsive flesh.

Lazily, he glanced from her to Stephanie. "Your partner doesn't seem too impressed by our work, Steph'nie," he drawled.

"Oh, I didn't mean to imply—Steffie's done a wonderful job!" Valerie blurted.

Her cheeks heated as he threw back his tawny head and laughed. Part of her blush was due to the implications of her remark, but the other part was the glorious sound of C. C. Wyatt's laughter.

"So she has," he remarked. His gaze still on Valerie's rosy face, he put new creases in his hat. "Steph'nie, you mind if I borrow your partner awhile? Being a chauvinistic male oinker," he said with a sidelong glance at Stephanie, thereby causing her to pinken and Valerie to wonder sharply what private joke they shared, "I feel bound and determined to impress her with my work."

"Of course I don't mind. I'm going to be busy all afternoon, so borrow away, C.C." She glanced at Valerie. "That is, if she wants the doubtful pleasure of your company." She sniffed, and he laughed again.

Valerie straightened. "Stephanie, your being busy doesn't automatically preclude my presence. You don't have to entertain me, you know," she said in gentle reproof. "But I would like to see more of your work, C.C." A hint of a saucy smile tilted her lips. "After all, it never hurts to show an interest in a client's business."

This time *she* got that quirk of mouth and sidelong look through a thick fringe of lashes. She felt warmed by his and Stephanie's banter. Any affectionate respect shown her sister pleased her. She stood silently by while they exchanged a few more, rather crisp words concerning their time schedules. Then he put his hat back on and guided his choice of companion to his truck.

Valerie was acutely glad that she was his choice. *I feel like I've just been asked to the prom by the star of the football team,* she thought, wryly amused at her girlish fizz of pleasure.

Her smile ironic, she reminded herself that they were merely going to look at more construction sites.

As they passed by Stephanie's bronze-and-green pickup, Valerie commented, "Everyone drives pickups here. That's an exaggeration, I know, but not by much."

His grin dug a dimple in each tanned cheek. "This is Texas, honey. Pickup trucks and Stetsons, boots and barbecues. Not your usual Mississippi fare, I take it." His grin faded with a sharp glance her way. "I'm sorry, I didn't mean to call you 'honey.' Guess I got into the habit with Steph'nie and put the same handle on you. Sorry."

Valerie nodded. She was sorry, too, that his endearment didn't fit her as easily as it did her sister.

He opened the door for her and, in an unexpected move, put both hands to her waist and lifted her inside the high-riding truck. Her voice unsteady, she thanked him. She felt as if his fingerprints were branded on her skin.

While he seated himself beside her, she smoothed her full skirt. It suddenly seemed very close in the spacious cab.

She fumbled with the seat belt.

He shifted in his seat and leaned toward her. "Here, let me help you. That thing's still stiff and new."

His breath brushed her cheek as he leaned closer to manipulate the unyielding strap. She could feel his body heat and smell the cologne on his clean-shaven cheek.

Why was she so *aware* of him?

The seat belt yielded and he guided it down across her thigh to the equally stiff clasp. When it clicked, he raised his head and let his gaze touch her parted lips before connecting with her eyes. She was caught in their boundless blue depths, caught and held while the small space between their bodies snapped with sexual tension.

Slowly he drew back. She drew a tremulous breath.

"Thank you," she said.

He curled his fingers around the steering wheel. "You're welcome." He drove onto the street before asking, "What part of Mississippi are you from?"

"Clinton. It's a lovely little town on the outskirts of Jackson."

"Steph'nie says you're thinking of moving here."

"Most of that's wishful thinking on Stephanie's part," Valerie responded a little too tartly.

C.C.'s profile was impassive. "You like your own little part of the world, then."

"Oh, yes. Some of my favorite things are there. Magnolia trees, jasmine, sultry summer evenings..."

"We have the same things here."

"My home, my friends, my job... my memories."

He shifted and released a long breath. "Kind of hard to beat that. Unless, of course, you make a new home, new friends, new memories. That's what I've been trying to do. It isn't easy, but it's got to be done."

"I know," Valerie said over a lump in her throat. "I'm just not sure I want to, that's all. I could live quite contentedly with the way things are. Home and friends don't have to change, even if everything else does."

"You dislike change?"

"I used to love it. But now... it's just another challenge. And there are so many challenges."

She clasped her hands.

His big hand suddenly covered both of hers, jolting her.

"I know, I've felt that way, too," he said, his voice low and gruff. "Just stay in your snug little rut, park yourself there and to hell with the rest of the world. It doesn't work, though. The rest of the world won't let it. How long have you been a widow?"

Unable to resist, she let her fingers relax under his big, comforting hand. He drove competently with just one.

"Almost three years now. It sounds like a long time, doesn't it? But sometimes it feels like only yesterday."

When he removed his hand, she felt a tiny chill. Resolutely, she ignored it.

"How long has it been for you?" she asked softly.

"A few months longer."

Although his voice was matter-of-fact, she heard a tremor in it and her heart went out to him. He'd known the same brutal emotions as she, felt the same tearing sense of desolation of a gentle world gone horribly awry.

No, not quite the same, she reflected coldly, sliding her hand up her chest to her throat. Not quite.

But the brief look they shared softened her heart again as she glimpsed the haggard face he would have hidden from everyone but himself. Nevertheless her tone was cool.

"Did you love her terribly much?"

"Oh, yes, I loved her. She was my world, she and Andy. Our son. They were both killed instantly, a head-on collision."

Valerie lowered her head as her eyes misted. "Dreadful," she said simply.

"Yes, it was that."

They were silent for a time, each lost in their own, very similar thoughts. She wondered if he was as taken aback as she at their intimate conversation. Ordinarily she was reticent about her personal feelings. But talking like this with him seemed so natural. For him, too?

Beneath her lashes she studied the strong fingers wrapped loosely around the steering wheel. Unbidden, her mind created images of them moving over a woman's body...her body. Valerie, really now, she scolded herself, doggedly amused at her fantasizing.

Amused derision was very helpful in relieving the niggling anxieties he aroused.

Very shortly he turned onto a wide parkway that boasted a large red metal sculpture at its entrance. "Never have been able to figure that out," he admitted. "I'm sure it has a meaning, but what it is beats me."

"Me, too." Valerie studied it as they drove past. Did he like art? Was he knowledgeable in such things? It was astonishing how much she wanted to know about this man. She already knew that she liked him. That was odd in itself; they had only spent a short evening together and talked in generalities. But then he was an extremely likeable man. We could even be friends, she thought.

That's why she found him so interesting, of course. One wanted to know all about a person if one liked him as a friend.

At length she asked, "Where are we going?"

"Just down the road a piece. Several builders, including myself, are planning next year's Parade of Homes. You familiar with that?"

She shook her head. Her hair was loose, and the silky brown locks swayed gently. Silver-and-turquoise earrings dangled from her earlobes. The flux of motion caught C.C.'s eye again and he smiled at her.

"It's simple enough. We each build a house or two in a specific price range—spec houses, which means houses built on speculation rather than contract—and open them to the public for several weeks, hopefully to sell them during that time, usually in March." He paused and shot her another glance. "The price range this year will start at a quarter of a million dollars."

Valerie shot *him* a glance. Was he trying to impress her? If so, he'd succeeded.

She whistled. "A quarter of a million dollars for a spec house? Will the market bear that kind of price?"

"Around here it will. Funny enough, the more expensive houses are the ones that sell easier in a depressed market. But we're coming back from our downward tailspin," he said with such confident pride that she gave a delighted little laugh.

"I like your laugh," he said. "Here we are. At least, here we are at the tract we've chosen. Would you like to see the plans? They're still rough, no one's locked in yet," he went on when she nodded, "but this will give you some idea of what I'm talking about."

He pulled to the side of the road and retrieved a rolled-up paper from his briefcase. Unsnapping his seat belt, he shifted closer. Their shoulders touched as she helped him unfold the long blueprint. Again she felt that disconcerting tingle. This time it radiated down her entire arm.

Determinedly she concentrated on the blueprint. Roughly sketched houses were marked according to owner, style and suggested price.

"This one is mine."

Valerie's gaze followed the long, tanned finger to a large bay-windowed home with a double front door, broad steps and a circular driveway. She looked up, entranced for a few seconds by the blueness of his eyes and the pride she saw there.

She pulled her gaze back to the blueprint. "C.C., I am impressed," she said. He shrugged, and she hid a smile. A few strokes of the pencil had fronted all the houses with handsome shrubs and trees. "Who's doing the landscaping on all these houses?"

"That'll be decided later."

"I certainly hope Ander's Nursery and Landscape will be in the running," she tossed off.

"If they want to compete, there's nothing stopping them." He restored the blueprints and brought the truck back onto the road. "How about a drink? I'm thirsty."

So was Valerie.

Instead of a restaurant, they stopped at a convenience store and bought two soft drinks.

"There's a lake out back, with ducks and stuff," he said offhandedly as they exited the store through a rear door. "Myself, I enjoy sitting out there."

Under the branches of an enormous willow tree, a rotating fan briskly stirred the hot, still air, inducing the sensation of a breeze. Beneath it, picnic tables had been placed on a small plank terrace. On the water, iridescent-hued mallard ducks and two white swans floated in the tree's shade. The forest of fluffy young pines rimming the lake helped to deepen the illusion of coolness.

She told him it was lovely.

"I knew you'd like it," he replied with a trace of smugness.

She narrowed her eyes. "You hoped I'd like it," she corrected, and was rewarded by his rich chuckle. She felt absurdly young and joyous.

The drinks were sweet and icy cold. Enjoying his, C.C. eyed her. "I was hoping you'd have dinner with me tonight, since I failed to receive a return invitation last night," he said with a beguiling touch of ruefulness.

Valerie wiped her mouth, a delaying tactic. She made a moue. "I'd really like to, but Stephanie may have something planned. So I'd better decline. But thank you, C.C."

C. C. Wyatt fought down his astonishingly strong disappointment. He should be relieved. He couldn't afford to become involved with this woman. She was too vulnerable.

Hell, *he* was too vulnerable. Vulnerable to those huge, lost dark eyes. For just a moment he'd seen the remnants of her pain and confusion, and it had tugged at heartstrings he'd long thought atrophied.

Watching her cross her long legs also tugged at strings located lower in his body. His mouth twisted. He could handle it. He wasn't a hormone-riddled teenager, even if he was feeling that way. But he didn't want anyone fooling around with his heart.

It was just as well, he told himself firmly, that she had declined his impulsive invitation.

But a willow frond played in her hair, brushing the russet strands in rhythm to the fan's air currents. Lacy sweeps of lashes concealed her eyes from him.

"Well, think about it a little, will you?" he growled. "I'm not asking you to join me in some deep, dark den of iniquity. I just hate to eat alone, that's all."

She glanced up at him, then glanced away. "You live alone?"

"Yes. I have a housekeeper, but she departs at six each evening and returns about ten the next morning. She's a pretty good cook, but I'm still sitting at that table by myself. How about you? Do you live with anyone?"

She felt his gaze upon her, fixedly intent. "Of course there are my children. And my mother-in-law, during the summer. The rest of the time she lives at a posh girls' boarding school in Louisiana. She's headmistress there, has been for twenty years. In fact, that's where my girls are now. They can start at ten, and she wanted so much for them to go there, at least for a year..."

Unthinkingly Valerie gave a telltale sigh. Granted, it was a privilege for her children to attend such a prestigious school. But she didn't like being away from them for such long periods of time. And a whole year... well, that was another decision to be made in the near future.

Becoming aware of C.C.'s alert gaze, she decided to change subjects. "I'm surprised you're living alone. You're a very attractive man."

"I don't have to," he conceded. "But I like it that way."

Valerie decided not to pursue that. A heavy silence fell between them. As he stretched his long legs, her gaze made an involuntary traverse down his flat stomach and taut, muscular thighs. A sparkler of warmth traveled from her heart all the way down to her toes.

His gaze seemed to penetrate her flesh, increasing the sensation as a long, tanned finger stroked idly down her arm. Was he aware of touching her? She doubted it. He looked distracted.

Abruptly he asked, "Want to take a walk?"

Valerie readily assented. A well-worn path circled the lake. Scattered along it were several children feeding the noisy flocks of ducks. Banks of fluffy clouds diluted the sun's force, and it would have been a pleasant walk if not for his brooding silence.

"What do you think of Steph'nie's boyfriend, Randy Bratton?" he asked with the same abruptness.

"I suppose he's nice enough. I've only met him three times. But she thinks the world of him," Valerie replied shortly. Why the odd note in his voice when he spoke of Stephanie's lover? Stephanie had said she and C.C. were just friends, and Valerie believed her. But was there a darker side to C.C.'s affection for her sister? An undercurrent of jealousy, perhaps?

"Yeah, I kind of guessed she did. You don't seem too bothered about it," he observed.

"Of course I'm not bothered," Valerie said with a quizzical look. "I'm glad she has someone, in fact."

C.C. grunted. "Well, it bothers me. I suppose they have some kind of 'understanding' that suits them fine, but it doesn't suit me. Maybe I'm just too old-fashioned, I don't know." He blew out a hard breath. "Or just think too much of her. Sometimes I look into those clear green eyes of hers and I'll be damned if I can see how she can tolerate the bastard. At first I thought she might not know he was already taken. But she's too smart to be fooled for this long a time. Not too smart to be foolish, but... Sometimes it's hard to keep my mouth shut. I know I got no business meddling in her affairs, but sometimes I just—"

Valerie stopped dead, her eyes widening as she comprehended what he was saying. "Wait a minute. Are you saying Randy Bratton is married?"

"Well, yeah. He's married. I thought you knew, Valerie. And approved, which I didn't much like—"

"No, I didn't know! And I certainly don't approve, I..." She shook her head in urgent denial. "No. You're mistaken, C.C., he's divorced. Stephanie said so, and you know Stephanie doesn't lie."

Her face was pale, her features taut. A muscle ticked in his jaw. "Then Steph'nie doesn't know."

Defeated, Valerie shot him a searching glance. "C.C., are you sure about this?"

"I'm sure."

Argumentative again, she planted her feet and faced him. "How are you sure? What makes you think such an awful thing?"

"I don't think, I know," he said in the tone of one unaccustomed to being doubted.

"How do you know, and when?"

"A couple of months ago, when I was going through some employee records. I don't always know a worker's background because I trust my foreman to do most of the hiring. No matter what Bratton's told her, he's a married man. And I think you feel the same way I do about that," C.C. said with an elating sense of relief.

"Yes, I do." Valerie walked on. "Why didn't you say something to her, at least try to stop her before she got in so deep!" she burst out.

"She's an intelligent, sophisticated adult who went into this with her eyes wide open," C.C. said with a level look. "At least that's what I thought. Besides, you want to guess what her reaction would be had I gone and stuck my nose into her private business?" he added so wryly that Valerie conceded a tiny smile.

"Yes, I can imagine, very easily. But I really don't think she knows," she said with a hard sigh. "She'll be crushed by this, just crushed."

He shrugged. "She'll get over it."

"Not that easily."

"Yes, that easily. She's too strong to let a paltry bit of heartache get the best of her."

"Paltry!" Valerie stopped again. "You're a cynic, C. C. Wyatt. And I don't like cynics." Turning abruptly, she headed back to the store.

Three

———

"Stephanie, I've decided to spend the rest of the afternoon at home looking over our account ledgers," Valerie said when she arrived back at the nursery.

"Oh. Well, sure," Stephanie replied. Her smooth brow wrinkled. "Val, is something wrong?"

Valerie knew her smile was strained; she could feel the tension in her facial muscles. "No, I just want to better acquaint myself with our business," she said, deliberately mistaking the question.

Just then a customer asked Stephanie for assistance, and Valerie went on to the office to pick up the ledgers.

C.C.'s revelations about Randy Bratton were heavy on her mind as she returned home. She and C.C. had not discussed the subject anymore. In fact, she'd been too angry and upset to discuss anything, and they had made the drive to the nursery in relative silence.

And at this point she had no idea what she meant to do about Stephanie's problem. A problem she didn't even know she had.

Well, the matter would simply have to be put aside until later, Valerie decided, when she could deal with it sensibly.

Luckily she knew how to compartmentalize, and apparently very well, too. At five o'clock a long roll of thunder broke her concentration. She looked at her watch with mild surprise. Her time had been well spent. She'd scrutinized their company records from January through today. She found nothing wrong, nor was she expecting to. But now she knew a little more about the day-to-day operation of a nursery and landscape firm.

In order to calculate the firm's growth rate, she would need last year's business sheets, too...

Her thoughts suddenly shifted to Randy Bratton. "That heel!" she muttered. Her hands clenched. How she'd love to wrap her fingers around his neck! Gracious, Valerie, getting a little bloodthirsty there, she chided herself, trying to moderate her dark mood.

But her attempt at amusement fell flat. With uncharacteristic roughness, Valerie slammed shut the ledger and stood so quickly her chair tipped over backward. Righting it, she strode to the telephone and dialed Stephanie's office.

"I'd like us to have dinner together tonight, Stephanie, just the two of us," she said. Her tone softened at Stephanie's startled question. "We just need to talk, that's all. In private, without all these other people running in and out. Come to think of it, why *do* we have all these people running in and out?"

"It gets lonesome in that big house at night, Val, so I have people around," Stephanie said defensively. "Not so much anymore now that I've got Randy, but still, I do get lonesome. Okay, we'll have a private evening for a change. I'll be home in about an hour. Let's just have a salad, I've pigged out today. Suit you?''

"Suits me," Valerie said. She wasn't hungry, she was too uptight to be hungry.

I'm not so lonely anymore since I've got Randy...

"Oh, God." Valerie sighed aloud. What on earth was she going to say to her sister? Honey, your boyfriend's a louse?

"Oh, she'd love me for that," Valerie muttered to herself. She was a little shocked to realize how very much she wanted her sister's love and Stephanie was bound to be furious at her.

Suddenly thrown into an agony of indecision, Valerie paced around the room. If she was wrong, and Stephanie already knew that Randy was married, then she would be on the defensive and quick to resent her big sister butting into her private life. And if she didn't know and was told by that same big sister...

Valerie sighed deeply. What she'd really like to do was bury her head in the sand. But she couldn't let such potentially damaging information just lay there—she had to act on it. When she did, she'd be putting their relationship in serious jeopardy, for of course the younger woman would be hurt and angry. Like as not, that anger would be directed at the bearer of bad news, not just the object of it.

Valerie knew this from personal experience. She had a friend who had found herself in the same miserable situation. Recalling that friend's hurt and embarrassment when she did find out evoked another deep sigh. By the time Stephanie walked in the door, Valerie had worked herself into a mass of nerves.

"Stephanie, sit down, please, we have to talk," she ordered more than requested.

Stephanie eyed her warily. "About what? What's wrong, Val? Have you decided not to move in with me?"

"No. Yes. I don't know. This isn't about that. Look, how well do you know Randy Bratton?"

"Very well, I think. Why?"

"And I think not. Stephanie, there's no easy way to put this. So I'll be blunt. Did you know Randy's married?"

"What?" Stephanie gave a choked laugh. "Val, for heaven's sake, what is this? Randy's divorced, I told you that."

"I know what you told me, what he's obviously told you. But he lied. He's not divorced. He's still a married man." Valerie caught her breath as her sister's face twisted with shock. "Honey, I know this is hard for you—"

"Hard for *me!*" Stephanie's eyes filled with hurt and tears. "Valerie, for God's sake—this is just...just plain nonsense. Randy wouldn't lie to me!" Anger contorted her delicate features. "He didn't lie, damn it! Why are you doing this to me, anyway!" she exploded. "Why are you trying to hurt me?"

Valerie threw her hands up in appeal. "Darling, I wouldn't try to hurt you, not deliberately. You had to know this, you had to be told, don't you see? He's no good for you—"

"He *is* good for me, and, no, I don't see!" Furiously Stephanie swiped at tears. "Where did you get this idea, anyway?"

Valerie drew a breath and let it out. Should she reveal C.C.'s involvement in this unhappy affair? No. That would open up a whole new area of embarrassment, for both parties. "I can't tell you that. But it's not just an idea. As much as I hate to say it, I truly believe Randy's deceived you."

Stephanie's face was a tight, tearstained mask. "And as much as *I* hate to say it, I think you've gotten ahold of an unfounded rumor and you're spreading it around. It's obvious you don't like Randy. Well, that's your problem, not mine!"

"Steffie—"

"I don't want to hear any more, Valerie!"

"All right. But do me a favor? Ask him."

"No, I won't ask him! I told you he's already said, loud and clear, that he *was* married, but that he is not *now* married," Stephanie said in hot, measured tones. "And I happen to believe him. Why shouldn't I? He has his own apartment—I've been there several times and there's never been the least suspicion of a wife in the picture!"

"Maybe she lives in another town, or even another state. Steffie, please, at least consider the possibility. You know I wouldn't just repeat an unfounded rumor..." Valerie began.

But Stephanie brushed past her with a choked, "I don't know any such thing. Now if you'll excuse me, I'm going out for the evening. Leave me alone, Val!" she cried warningly as Valerie ran after her.

The back door slammed. Seconds ticked by as Valerie waited. She heard the truck start up and mentally followed its progress down the drive to the street. Her shoulders slumped.

"She'll come around," she told herself, feeling a frantic need to believe that. "After the shock wears off, Stephanie will thank me."

But few people were grateful for such a shock. Fearful and confused, Valerie sat down on the couch and buried her face in her hands. What was she going to do? What *could* she do? Backtrack, tell Stephanie that she'd been mistaken and apologize for spreading gossip? Or put the blame on C.C., identify him as the source of her so-called gossip?

Quickly she rejected this easy solution. She didn't blame C.C. for her predicament. He had told her in all innocence.

Valerie drew her knees to her chest and hunched over in a painful knot of confusion. Her altercation with Stephanie was not limited to a matter of ill will between sisters. It cast a shadow on everything—the possibility of making a new home here, of creating a whole new life and becoming a vital part of Stephanie's. And C.C.'s . . .

She swiftly blocked that thought. C.C. didn't figure in this. True, she couldn't deny her attraction to him. But simple male and female chemistry was too common to be given much importance.

It was nice, though, to know she could still feel that lovely chemistry. Nice and unbothersome. She'd never had any trouble controlling her erotic desires.

Anxiety and misery had created kinks of tension in her shoulders. Standing, she massaged them as she firmed her decision. Whatever the cost to herself, she'd had no choice but to tell Stephanie.

"Steffie will come around," she repeated doggedly. "And when she does, we'll talk it through, like friends. Like sisters."

Seven o'clock came and went. Valerie bathed, washed her hair, anything to find tasks for her restless hands.

Eight o'clock.

She sat in the solarium and watched a distant lightning storm, wishing she had someone to talk to, someone to be with. C.C. The thought was a live ember in her mind. She hated to feel so needful. But she did.

Without conscious intent, driven by something she couldn't resist, she went to the kitchen, looked up his number and hurriedly dialed the phone.

His husky hello created a sense of airlessness. She felt an almost overwhelming desire to cry all over him. She swallowed, hard.

"Hi, C.C. This is Valerie. I've changed my mind. I'd like to see that little piano bar you spoke of. But if the hour's too late, I'll understand—"

"It's not at all too late. I'll pick you up in, say, twenty minutes?"

She released her breath. "That's fine. Thank you, C.C."

He chuckled. "You're welcome. Twenty minutes. Dress up, we're going to do some dancing."

Doubting that her mood would lend itself to dancing, Valerie nevertheless selected a flirty-skirted little black frock with long, slim sleeves. It was at least ten years old, but bore a designer label.

She donned her prosthesis with a moue of distaste. The bra, though black and lace trimmed, was ugly in her eyes. Only when she'd covered it with a slip did she turn to the mirror to finish dressing.

The dress was flattering to her willowy figure and slender arms. A gold bracelet with stones as smooth as raspberry ice encircled one slender wrist, and matching circlets adorned her ears. As usual, her hair was styled in a sleek chignon. She anchored it with a black velvet bow.

After slipping on satin pumps the color of her necklace, she surveyed herself in the floor-length mirror backing the closet door. She'd never been a typically pretty woman. Still, her gamine's smile and sculpted cheekbones had served her in good stead. Satisfied, she went to find a wrap.

The sky was ominously black when she opened the door to C. C. Wyatt. Removing his pearl-gray Stetson, he cocked his head and looked her up and down. His mouth crooked at the corners with a growing smile. His eyes danced.

"I sure do like those red shoes, lady."

"So do I," she returned dryly. Her spirits rose immediately. C.C. was a treat for feminine eyes in his soft blue linen shirt and gray suit tailored with a Western flair. He wore shining black alligator boots, she noted with a quick smile. *You're something of a dandy, C. C. Wyatt!*

She felt too fragile to ask him in. Even from where she was standing she could feel the current rippling between them. So she stepped outside and shut the door.

He offered his arm and she took it. He put his hand over hers. The touch made her senses jump.

"Mmm, you smell good. Like the blossoms of the moonflower vine."

Her nose wrinkled dubiously. She looked curious, uncertain, intrigued despite herself. "Thank you. But what on earth is a moonflower? Or is there any such thing?"

"Certainly there is. I have one growing by my terrace. It's a flower that only blooms during the dark hours of night. Smells like honey and roses and jasmine, all rolled up into one blossom. You need that on?" he asked, eyeing the shawl she carried.

"No, it's just for chilly clubs."

"What a shame. I'd have liked to help you into it."

Lord, that jaunty tilt of head and rakish grin! "I'd have liked you to help me into it."

She bit her lip. Was she flirting with him?

"We can remedy that. The night's getting chillier by the minute."

He frowned, hearing his low words. Was he flirting with her?

"C.C., I'd very much like to have you for a friend," she said in subtle warning.

C.C. bit back the angry retort that sprang from his well-fleshed ego. It had been a long time since a woman had merely wanted his friendship. But her soft little plea had gotten to him. She needed to feel safe.

"I'd like to be your friend," he replied quietly.

"Listen, I'm not all that much of cynic," he said, scowling into her piquant face. "When I spoke of Steph'nie's *heartache* being paltry, I wasn't saying she was shallow. I was applying it to the measure of the man she's involved with.''

After a moment, a faint smile touched her lips. "In that case, you're *not* cynical."

"Well, maybe I am a little bit, but that comes with age."

"So it does." Valerie put her hand on his. Her fingers looked like slim white ribbons on his skin.

Huge, fat raindrops splashed the sidewalk. "Guess we'd better run for it," he said, and grabbed her hand.

Absurdly glad that she smelled good, Valerie "ran for it," *it* being a long, black Lincoln Town Car.

"Can't even get my legs into one of those little bitty cars," he informed her when she commented on its size.

She laughed, feeling easy with him now that she'd defined their relationship. As the rain increased, he turned on the wipers, a simple act that enclosed them in a very small, cozy world. She watched him from the corners of her eyes. The dimple in his cheek flickered at some personal amusement.

It flickered again, a fingertip enticement. "C.C...." She cleared her throat. "While I'd appreciate music, I'm really not in a dancing mood. You see..."

She paused. Should she tell him about her scene with Stephanie? No. It was private. Besides, she didn't want to get serious about anything tonight. If he didn't mention it, she wouldn't.

"I spent all afternoon going over our books and I'm rather stiff and tired," she finished smoothly.

"You know, dancing does a lot for tired, stiff bones," he remarked. "But if you'd rather listen than participate, the bar features a fine singer."

Valerie agreed that sounded wonderful. They didn't have to dance to enjoy the piano bar.

Except that they did, of course. He wouldn't hear of letting a good dance floor go to waste.

"One dance," she relented. But even as she reluctantly gave in, she chided herself for the fraud she undoubtedly was. She wanted to feel his arms around her, more than just wanted. Her desire to be held had become an aching need.

He didn't disappoint her. Like all big, sensitive men, he was aware of his own strength. Slowly, carefully, he drew her into his embrace.

C.C. was indeed aware of his size. He held her as he would a tender blossom. He had embraced delicately fashioned women before, but this one—ah, this one—was fine-boned delicacy on a scale that electrified his senses.

He felt the swift, hot thrust of desire with a kind of exultation. He had always been a virile man, but for the past few years his desires seemed limited to a basic roil of heat in his loins. With Valerie, it rampaged all over him. From his brain, to his heart, to the soles of his feet, he knew he was holding a warm, desirable woman in his arms.

A low, husky laugh escaped his lips. Valerie wondered at it. But wonder changed texture as his embrace tightened. The light brush of bodies flooded her with lovely sensations. His cheek came to rest on hers and she drew a deep breath of him. His mustache brushed her earlobe and she quivered. Soft music and dim lights, combined with the scent and feel of a very masculine male, seemed to pour into her as if she were a crystal vase.

Just dancing again, with a man who was an expert at it, gifted her with the kind of joyous pleasure she'd always loved so much. Romantic, she thought longingly. It had been years since she'd felt the beauty of romance, or had to resist this sweet temptation to move into the muscled warmth of a man's body.

Relaxing, she let herself drift with the moment. It was dangerous, but irresistibly so.

C.C. lifted his head. "Valerie, I'm sorry about this afternoon. My intention was not to make you mad, believe me."

A mindless spear of resentment stabbed her as the scene with Stephanie suddenly crashed back into her mind. Why did he have to bring that up right now?

"And I'm sorry I got so huffy. Okay?" she asked lightly.

A chuckle graveled his voice. "Okay, lady."

His cheek pressed to hers again, but the moment was ruined. When the music stopped, Valerie gave herself a sharp mental shake to dislodge any remaining desire to continue this. It was the kind of madness she couldn't risk.

"More wine?" C.C. asked, smiling as she assented. No table trash for Valerie Hepburn; she knew her wines. He was just damn glad he knew a little bit about wine, too. "You know, when we were first introduced, I thought, 'Valerie Hepburn. Now that's an adorable name.'"

Valerie felt herself blushing. "Adorable? At thirty-nine? I don't know about that, C.C. But thanks for the thought."

C.C. leaned across the little table. "So tell me about adorable Valerie."

"Well, for one thing, she doesn't want any more wine, she'd like an Irish coffee, please. For another, I think she was a pretty grand girl at one time. Right after high-school graduation she left Maryland to bum around Europe for a year. She—I—enrolled in college there, went a year, met Robert, my husband, got married, lived in Paris—all by the age of twenty. A busy two years!" She laughed.

She paused to allow him to order her coffee. For himself C.C. requested a glass of sparkling water. Lazy blue eyes held hers captive. "And then?"

"And then I became bored, went to work at Christian Dior doing piecework, moved to the country, and nine years later gave birth to twin daughters. Then my husband's job ceased to be, so we moved back to his Mississippi hometown and started an accounting firm. I had to get my degree, of course, which I did... Then he died. A heart attack." Valerie took a sip of wine. "End of story."

Unless you count a modified mastectomy.

"It's not the end of story," C.C. rebuked. "Life goes on, whether you're here or there. Although I hope it will be here." His mouth curled humorously. "I don't have many women I can call good friends."

"I can guess why. Very few women would be satisfied with just your friendship, especially if you decided to turn up the heat," Valerie said frankly. The icy stiffness that had coated her just moments before melted under his roguish grin. So full of himself, she thought, liking him even more. "I don't have that many men I call good friends, either. That ought to make a nonsexual friendship all the more precious, I'd think."

Giving her a level look, C.C. agreed it should. "But there are such things as sexual friendships, which can be even more precious."

"Oh, yes." For just a second her eyes grew dreamy. "But they're very rare."

"And very glorious," he murmured, a faraway look in his eyes.

Silence fell around them like a soft cloak.

Their drinks came. She sipped hers. "Wonderful," she told him. "C.C., stop me if I get too personal, but I wondered why you and Jordan are estranged. If he's your only surviving son, then surely..." She let it trail away.

C.C. rubbed the back of his neck. "My fault, mostly. Look, it's a long story and not a pretty one, either. So let's just say I'm to blame and let it go at that."

"If you wish, but my interest is genuine. I like to know all about my friends."

Eyes glinting, he sat back. "Overdoing this friendship bit a little, aren't you?"

"No, I don't think so. Unless, of course, you're playing games with me."

His mouth twisted, wagging his mustache. "Valerie, in all honesty I'd be delighted to play games with you. But I was sincere about being your friend. I'd hate not to be, in fact."

Her laughter bubbled up. "Thank you. I think. I also think I'll have another Irish coffee."

It was past eleven when she felt the onset of emotional fatigue. She glanced at her watch. "It's getting late, C.C. This has been a lovely evening, but I'd like to get on home now," she said, thinking of Stephanie, wondering where she was. Home? Or out in this black, stormy night? She desperately hoped that she wasn't coming home to an empty house.

Stephanie's truck wasn't in the carport. Beneath her shawl, Valerie clenched her hands to contain her disappointment. Rain was sluicing down the car windows, and C.C. chose to stop beneath the empty shelter. They dashed to the back porch, grateful for the covered archway.

Valerie stood quietly by while he unlocked and opened the door. He was so near she could smell the clean scent of raindrops on his hair. She knew he wanted to kiss her, and she wanted to be kissed. But the almost liquid warmth in the pit of her stomach told her what kind of kiss it would be, and of the complications that could follow. Compromising, she stretched up and touched her lips to his cheek.

He turned his head a little, and her lips rested briefly at the corner of his mouth. She prayed he wouldn't go any further. Her state of mind was rapidly deteriorating, and she didn't trust herself right now.

He didn't move, although one hand came up to cradle the back of her head with a feathery, nonpressuring touch. The moment seemed to spin out on silvered threads of tension. Her toes trembled. This aching desire to slide her mouth onto his curled into a hot, bright knot in her stomach.

"God!" she heard him whisper.

Then his hand fell away. Breathing again, her lips tingling with their brief taste of C. C. Wyatt, she drew back.

"Mr. Wyatt, I'm dying of curiosity. What does 'C.C.' stand for?"

He grinned. "Christopher Charles Wyatt," he said. With that, he kissed her nose and dashed out into the rain again.

Valerie locked the door behind her and leaned against it. Christopher Charles Wyatt. She liked his name. It suited him.

She hurried down the hall. Stephanie's empty bedroom evoked a frown. Valerie sensibly told herself there was nothing to be done about it. But that didn't stop her from worrying. She didn't know Stephanie well enough to predict just how she'd react when she came home. But it wouldn't be pleasant.

With disturbing ease, she diverted her thoughts to C. C. Wyatt and their evening together. A fiery little shiver swept through her heart and body. Odd, she thought, how many small feelings he stirred up. But she didn't mind, as long as they stayed small.

The next morning was windy and overcast. "Oh, great," Valerie muttered. She hadn't slept well, and the gray light filtering through her windows didn't help any.

She fervently hoped it wouldn't rain. C.C.'s job was to be finished up today. Feeling groggy and dispirited, she passed by Stephanie's empty bedroom with a worried frown. Hadn't she come home at all last night?

A search of the house revealed Stephanie and her cat asleep in the solarium. Her pale face was stained with tears. Even in sleep, her tender mouth drooped at the corners.

Her heart twisting with pain, Valerie went to the kitchen to prepare the coffee she'd forgotten to make last night.

When it was ready, she fixed a tray and carried it back to the solarium. "Stephanie? Time to get up."

Stephanie awoke instantly. Without comment she accepted the proffered cup of coffee. She sipped it, grimaced, then rubbed her reddened eyelids. "Damn," she muttered, running a hand over her forehead. "I had a few drinks last night."

"Oh, Stephanie, honey, you could have been hurt!"

"I'm not that dumb. Some friends drove me and my truck home. Anyway, I was already hurt. Last night when I stormed out of here, I went to Randy's apartment. I asked him about... what you said. I didn't want to, but I didn't seem to have any choice," she said bitterly. "I couldn't get it out of my mind."

Her lashes shot up to reveal anguished green eyes. "He admitted it. He's still married. Separated, but still, like you said, a married man. So I split. I hope you're satisfied, Val."

"Satisfied? Stephanie, you can't believe that! I'd have given anything to spare you—"

"Then spare me this, too, all right?" Stephanie said, getting up. "I don't need your pity."

"It's commiseration, not pity. Please, we need to talk." Valerie reached out to her, but Stephanie twisted aside.

"No, I don't want to talk," she choked out. "I just want to forget about it, all right?" Raging green eyes impacted with Valerie's. "Just don't even bring it up again."

Valerie bowed her head. She hurt so much for her sister she wanted to weep. "If that's what you really want, darling."

"It's what I want. Now if you'll excuse me, I have to get ready for work. Thanks for the coffee."

"You're welcome. I'll come down to the nursery with you."

"Don't bother. Today won't be very busy."

"I'll come, anyway. There's bound to be something I can do."

"Suit yourself," Stephanie said, and went to her room.

She really does hate me, Valerie thought wretchedly. But it's just for now, when she's hurting so. Later it will be all right. She walked to her own room remembering all the other times she'd clung to that restorative thought.

The day passed with trying slowness, giving Valerie cause to doubt her trusty panacea. Although there was no overt sign of animosity between the two sisters as they worked together, Stephanie was coolly polite. There were circles around her eyes, her smile was fixedly constant.

As much as it stung, Valerie could not help but be proud of her sister's valiant composure.

That evening Stephanie went out again. At least she didn't slam the door this time, Valerie thought with wan humor.

She glanced at the telephone, then shook her head. C.C. hadn't called her. But there was no reason why he should. She might have put a sparkle in his eye last night, but men his age usually preferred younger women.

Valerie vented a hard sigh. Maybe she'd better just avoid him altogether. She'd known him two days and already she was embroiled in dissension. Maybe she ought to avoid everything, she mused bitterly. Just pack up and go home, forget the future and whatever decisions she might have made...

Her jaw set. She wasn't a quitter. She'd stay here and see this thing through to the bitter end.

Then she'd go home.

Four

The first thing C. C. Wyatt put on each morning was his watch. After doing so, he folded his hands beneath his neck and stretched every hard-earned muscle in his long, lean frame.

These few extra minutes in bed were usually an enjoyable way to start his mornings. And usually he spent them rehashing the prior day's business and planning this one.

This day, however, his mind wouldn't stick to business. All he kept rehashing was the feel of Valerie Hepburn in his arms, the softness of her, the sweet, brief taste of her lips.

Almost a kiss. Not quite a kiss. One little move and he would have known the fullness of that honeyed mouth. But he hadn't made that move. Even though he wanted to so much that every muscle was strained in the tension of holding himself in check...

This was getting him nothing but stirred up. Never mind the other questions flitting through his mind. Why did she change her mind about being with him last night? Did she feel this touch of living fire, too?

Grunting, he moved off the bed and went into the bathroom. He turned on the shower massage until needles of water peppered his body, cooling his passions and raising more questions. It would have been so easy to open up to her last night. He didn't know why he'd been so tempted. He hadn't before. Certainly not by a stranger.

He shook his wet head. Valerie wasn't a stranger. She hadn't been from the moment he'd met her. Still, his relationship with his son, or lack of it, was his own business.

Stephanie wasn't. Closing his eyes, he lifted his chin and let the water beat against his face. He had pondered her problem and resolved nothing. Should he tell her that her lover was married? What did Valerie want him to do? He didn't want to make her all mad again, but neither could he dump something like this on her and then wash his hands of it.

Maybe he should have brought this all up last night. But he had sensed how oddly fragile their relationship was, and he didn't want to disrupt it further. And maybe Valerie thought it family business, which he should keep his nose out of—hell, who knew? Sometimes women were baffling mysteries as well as delicious delights.

Emerging from the shower, he knotted a towel around his hips and padded into the bedroom to turn on the television. Flash-flood alerts, more precipitation in the forecast. He pulled the drapes and found a rain-drenched landscape. Water ran ankle deep on both sides of the street and made shallow lakes in some of the yards.

His mood plummeted. He couldn't for the life of him think of a plausible reason to drop by Ander's Nursery on a day like this.

C.C. found a reason when he checked out his medical building later that morning. The grounds were awash with water. Plants and shrubs bobbed in the shin-deep current, and one of the trees had fallen despite anchoring guy wires. Well, Stephanie would just have to get back out here and clean up this mess, he thought sternly. He was such a softy where women were concerned that he had to be extra tough with her.

He, himself, wasn't exactly thrilled by the situation. But it did give him cause to confer with the two sisters. Deciding that it would be kinder to do it in person than over the telephone, he drove to the nursery.

When he arrived, C.C. took time to smooth his hair and straighten his Stetson before getting out. His manner was confident, almost insouciant, as he reached the combination shop and showroom. He opened the door, stepped inside—and stopped with a jarring breath.

"Upon a couch of flowers," Emily Dickinson had written. He couldn't recall the next line, but it might well have been that Valerie sat there.

There was an old-fashioned wicker settee covered with flowering plants. She was seated in their midst, her shining head bent to the invoice she checked so assiduously. A scattering of wispy dark curls framed the vulnerable, mother-of-pearl flesh of her nape, inducing a tenderness so potent that his breath tangled in his throat.

Stephanie was working behind the counter. Hurriedly he glanced at her, certain that the tremor that shook his powerful frame was visible. But neither woman had noticed him yet.

As Stephanie approached her with another sheaf of invoices, he heard Valerie say, "We both skipped breakfast, Steffie. Why don't we get a bite to eat?"

"You go if you want," came Stephanie's dispassionate reply. "I'm too busy right now."

Watching them, C.C. crushed the crown of his already battered hat. It was easy to see they were at odds with each other, and it didn't take much effort to guess the reason. Valerie had told her sister about Randy. And whether or not Stephanie believed it, she resented it furiously.

C.C. swore and jammed his hat back on his head. Just minutes ago he had decided to do the distasteful task himself, and now it was too late. Under his breath he cursed his delaying action. He'd wanted to spare her this. He'd wanted to be the *hero,* damn it!

Hurt flooded Valerie's dark eyes before she lowered her head again. He felt something clench inside him, like a fist. Fighting a dangerous surge of anger, he caught Stephanie's gaze, jerked his head toward the covered veranda and backed away from the door.

Though she looked puzzled, Stephanie made no comment as she slipped away from her sister. As soon as she moved onto the veranda, C.C. caught her arm and towed her farther down its pottery-studded length.

"What's going on with you and Valerie?" he demanded roughly. "And don't tell me it's nothing," he added as she started to do just that. "She told you about Randy, didn't she?"

"You know about that?" Stephanie jerked away, her eyes hot and glittery, her tone devoid of its usual respect. "Does everyone else on the job know, too?"

"No, everyone else doesn't know. Steph'nie, I know it hurts, but why are you taking it out on Valerie? Because she's the one who told you? Well, let me tell *you* something. I'm the one you should be angry with!"

Her eyes widened. "You? Why?"

"Because I'm the one she got it from in the first place. If you're going to be mad at someone, then be mad at me!" In a quieter tone, he went on. "Listen, honey, she came by the news innocently. I thought you knew, and had told her, I swear I did. And the reason I mentioned it is because I . . . well, I didn't like the situation. I was afraid you'd get hurt real bad, honey,'' he hurriedly explained as her chin whipped up. ''Lord knows I didn't mean to drive a wedge between you two. I was going to tell you myself, but she beat me to it.''

''How long have you known?'' she asked without inflection.

''For a while. I didn't think it was my place to say anything to you. I mean, I thought you had your eyes open, but Valerie knew better. Women usually do.'' He touched her shoulder. ''We were both thinking of your welfare, Steph'nie. You have to believe that.''

She didn't answer. C.C. knew from the set of her mouth that he hadn't swayed her. Valerie had shattered her illusions.

He had to clench his hands to restrain his frustrated need for action. He wanted this resolved right now, and resolved in Valerie's favor. But he doubted either woman would welcome his interference. You've already done enough harm. A regular bull in a china shop, he berated himself.

''You've got another problem far more worthy of attention than this uproar over a worthless bum,'' he said disgustedly.

Chilly green eyes flickered to his. ''Oh? And what's that?''

''Your job, that's what.'' His senses jumped as Valerie came out the door. Gladness flashed across her face before she veiled her expression. Vaguely happy, he snatched off his hat and smiled at her. She looked so good in jeans and a tailored pink shirt.

''Good morning Valerie.''

Her mouth tilted in quick response. ''Morning, C.C. What's all this about?'' she asked.

''I just came from the job your crew finished yesterday,'' he said. ''There's been some flash flooding and the whole place is underwater. Not my building, it sits up too high. But your plants are."

"But they're still in place?" Stephanie asked.

"No." His gaze shifted to her. "It's an unholy mess out there right now, and my clients sign the move-in papers tomorrow afternoon."

She bit her lip and C.C. swore again. His soft spot for distressed women was more than a handicap, it was a royal pain in the neck.

"Don't worry, C.C., we'll take care of it," Valerie stated.

"I'm banking on that," he said evenly.

Stephanie's jaw tightened. "We'll also honor the penalty clause for delay in completion of the job—"

A wave of hand chopped off her sentence. "Ordinarily I'd expect that, but this qualifies as an act of God, which does tend to absolve us both of responsibility," he added, dry humored.

"That's nice of you, C.C.," Valerie said stiffly, "but we can't accept—"

"It's all right, Val, this isn't a personal favor," Stephanie interrupted. "Thank you, C.C."

"You're welcome. Wish I could get off so easily, but looks like I've got drainage ditches to dig. I'll put off the signing until Monday," he said with characteristic brusqueness. "You can't work out there until it dries up a bit, and more rain is predicted for tonight."

Her face impassive, Stephanie thanked him again and excused herself.

C.C. mauled his hat some more. "Valerie, I'm sorry about this thing between you and Steph'nie. I hate for you two to be on the outs over a liar like Randy Bratton. I really did mean to tell her myself, but the right moment never seemed to come along."

"It wasn't your job to tell her, C.C., it was mine. And we're not on the outs, not exactly. She just has to sort herself out, that's all," Valerie said with touching bravado.

The wind plucked strands of hair from her chignon and spun them around her face. It flattened soft pink linen around her breasts. As if a floodgate had lifted, he felt desire spill through him again. She had beautiful breasts. High and proud and perky, he thought. Raising a hand to her hair, he brushed tendrils from her face, then ruefully shook his head as the wind promptly undid his efforts.

She shied from his touch, and he dropped his hand.

"You looked real pretty sitting there on that couch among all those flowers," he said, and then—of all the dumb things to do—he quoted that line of poetry to her.

She smiled, her unhappiness shoved aside, at least momentarily, by pleased interest. "You like poetry? So do I. Who's your favorite poet?"

"Dickinson, Keats…Robert Louis Stevenson, of course. His 'Windy Nights' used to scare me to death when I was a kid. Still raises my neck hairs when I hear it. But I read a little of everything."

As he spoke, he turned his hat around and around by its brim. Her gaze dropped to his moving fingers. "Who taught you to like poetry?"

"My mother," he said gruffly. He shifted. "Would you like to take in a movie tonight?" he asked with telling abruptness.

"Thank you, but I think I'd better hang around the house tonight. Stephanie may need me," she explained. "But I would like a rain check?"

"You've got it. She is breaking off with him, isn't she?" he asked tersely.

"I think she already has. But C.C., I'd prefer that we not discuss Stephanie's personal problems. We've already said enough and I don't think she'd like it."

C.C. frowned. He wanted to discuss the vexing matter, if for no other reason than to offer Valerie moral support.

"I doubt she would, either," he reluctantly agreed.

The rain stopped about two. When Stephanie returned from C.C.'s job site, Valerie asked gravely, "How did it look out there? As bad as C.C. said?"

"Pretty bad. The water's gone down, leaving a blanket of bark mulch from one end of the site to the other. It'll all have to be raked up after we replace the plants. I hate delaying C.C.'s signing."

"Steffie, it wasn't our fault. He said there were flash floods all over the area." That "our" had come so quickly, Valerie thought with a bleak smile. "Can I help you with that unpacking?"

"No, I can do it. There's another bunch of invoices in the office, if you'd like to get started on them."

Stephanie spoke with no discernible emotion. Nodding, Valerie retraced her steps to the office.

At five-thirty, looking around the nearly empty nursery, she suggested going home to prepare dinner. "How many people are you bringing home tonight?" she asked, injecting a teasing note into her voice.

Stephanie's smile was brief. "None. I'm going out tonight. I'm leaving straight from the nursery, so you might as well go on home." She hesitated as Valerie's eyes clouded. "Val, I'm hurting," she said softly, angrily. She turned, her slender back stiff and rejecting.

Grateful for even this small break in the wall her sister had thrown up between them, Valerie touched her shoulder. "I know. And I should have minded my own business. I'm here if you need me."

There was no response other than a small twitch of a muscle beneath her fingers.

Shortly afterward Valerie decided to take her sister's suggestion and go on home. Just back to an empty house, actually, she thought, unlocking the door.

Despite its cheerful furnishings and peach-colored walls, her bedroom felt dark and cold and her footsteps seemed to echo. She missed her children, her home, the light and laughter that had once surrounded her. She felt like crying for no reason, for a hundred reasons.

She took off the bra and massaged the tiny welt beneath her breast. Apparently she'd gained a little weight indulging her passion for cooking, and the garment was too snug around her midriff. Another reason to hate the contraption, she thought irrationally.

She bathed, and shampooed her hair, dried it, piled it atop her head. The clock ticked loudly. Nothing on television, she discovered. Nibbling on a pretzel, she eyed the telephone. Logic fought with temptation for a violent moment. Temptation won.

She dialed C.C.'s number, then nearly hung up as it rang. This was the second time she'd said no to his invitation, then changed her mind. Would he mind? And what if he'd already made other plans for the evening?

"Hello?"

She sank into a chair as his husky voice caressed her ear.

"C.C.? Valerie. I was wondering if I could pick up that rain check on a movie? I'm free after all."

"Steph'nie gone out again?"

"Yes. She doesn't seem to have much use for an older sister right now," Valerie said starkly. She heard his whispered curse. "I understand, though," she added quickly. "It just takes time. Well, am I in luck, or have you already found someone else for tonight?" she asked on a lighter note.

There was a slight pause. Then he chuckled. "You're in luck. We'll have to hurry, though, it starts in fifteen minutes."

"We'll never make it," she fretted. "How about you coming here? We have some old movies in our video collection—*The African Queen,* with Bogie and Hepburn. How does that sound? Or don't you like old movies?"

"Oh, yes, I like old movies," he replied, making it sound like an intimate communion, she thought. A breathlessness assailed her as her spirits took off like startled birds.

"Good," she said briskly. "Half an hour?"

"Suits me." His voice was soft, husky. "Can I bring something, some wine, perhaps?"

"No, thank you, we have plenty." Valerie bit her lip; she didn't mean to sound so stiff! But her reaction to his simple inquiry was idiotically strong. She ended the conversation with a sprightly, "See you in thirty minutes," and hung up with a whoosh of breath.

Trying, hopelessly, not to read too much into her bold action as well as its delightful consequence, Valerie sped down the hall to her room. She put on a fresh prosthesis, drew on satin panties. Flowing peacock-blue trousers with apple-green cuffs and a matching tunic enhanced her willowy figure. She tied the braided blue-and-green sash loosely, yet her bosom thrust seductively against the soft fabric. A sham, she thought. An empty facade. She clasped her hands between the full swells as she recalled Stephanie's question. *Why didn't you consider reconstruction?*

There had been any number of reasons, including fear, but the main one was her answer to Stephanie. It simply hadn't mattered.

At the time she'd undergone surgery, she had felt shattered anew by loss, certain, in her devastated frame of mind, that that part of her life was over. She would never remarry; how could it matter?

But for just a moment, before she pushed the subject back into its secretive nook, she realized something. Applied to now, this minute, her answer was no longer true. C.C. had made it matter.

Shivering, she thrust that thought aside, too. She had no intention of becoming intimately involved with C. C. Wyatt!

Nebulously angered, she told herself that the long-dormant feelings he had awakened were natural, and in no way represented a major flaw in her defenses. Then, with an affirmative pat on her topknot, she returned to the den and rummaged through Stephanie's video tapes until she found the one she wanted.

C.C. drove automatically. His attention was focused inward, on the feelings storming his big frame. Gladness. Mingled desire and hope. Her call had started his heartbeat on a different rhythm and it was still too fast to be comfortable.

He had started to say no to her. But he couldn't. He wanted to see her too much. An oath escaped him as he took a curve too fast. He wished he didn't feel so eager to get there. It was hard to keep within the speed limit.

With a certain amount of alarm, he reminded himself of his determination not to get emotionally involved, with any woman. There were too many pitfalls, too many chances to get hurt. But they were two mature adults. Very mature. Both could handle a simple sexual affair.

If it remained that way. He gave his head a decisive shake. It would—he'd see to that. If it ever got started. She was wary, he knew that. Well, so was he. All the more reason to confine this to a simple, uncomplicated affair. When she opened the door to him, his heart jumped into his throat.

"You look almost edible," he said, sighing.

Valerie hoped she thanked him properly. A pulse was hammering urgent messages in her ears. He was dressed very casual tonight, in a red, open-throated knit sweater and lean black corduroy slacks. Dampness had dropped a wing of hair over his forehead. Every time he shoved it back, it returned to its chosen place. Her fingers itched to smooth the rumpled lock.

She brushed at her tunic, unconsciously flattening it against her sleek thighs. The misty flush of excitement spread to her ivory neck as he followed her to the kitchen. They bantered back and forth while she prepared wine and popcorn to go with their movie, his eyes bright and constantly upon her.

To have a man in the kitchen telling her about his day while she prepared food! Valerie had forgotten this simple but enormous pleasure. A lump formed in her throat as she responded to the warmth and well-being it engendered.

C.C. thought he could stay here forever, sitting on a bar stool watching a woman's comely movements about the brightly lit room. Just soaking up pure pleasure, he thought, laughing for no reason at all, except that he felt so good.

They moved on to the den and he sat down on the couch.

"I really enjoyed the piano bar the other night, C.C.," she said, handing him a glass of wine.

"So did I." He tasted the wine, smiled at its fine quality, let his gaze do a slow waltz down her silk-covered body. "You're a wonderful dancer, Ms. Hepburn. Light as a flower in my arms."

He stared at her for a contemplative second. Then, as if coming to a decision, he set down his wine. "Last night I had trouble sleeping because of you. I kept wondering how that mouth of yours would taste. When you called tonight, I started to say no because I had decided you were right, that we should keep this friendship simple. But then I changed my mind. Because, you see, I had to *know* how that lovely mouth would taste. And I will, before this evening's over."

Her lips twisted. "Be still, my foolish heart," she quipped, but her eyes gave her away and she knew it. Her voice cooled. "Have I anything to say about this?"

C.C.'s gaze wandered over her face. A tiny black velvet mole sat, as if placed by hand, high on one sculpted cheekbone. Placed there to entice a man's mouth, he thought with a little thrill of anticipation. Excitement beat in his blood, and just over the prospect of one kiss. Amazing, he mused, absurdly delighted at the innocence in that.

Slowly he brought his eyes up to hers. "Not a thing."

"You may find you're wrong about that." Valerie wet her dry throat with a sip of wine. His smile was confident. It both annoyed and stimulated at once. "Very wrong."

He cocked his head. "I may, hmm?"

"You may."

"You mean there's a chance that all I've got to look forward to is another miserable night spent *wondering?*"

He looked so comically appalled at the thought that Valerie burst out laughing. A second later, he joined her and the sound was music to her ears. Relaxing, she willed herself to ignore her anxious little flutterings and just enjoy the big, personable male.

She sat down beside him on the couch and picked up the remote control. Their knees touched as he shifted around to face her. He stretched out an arm behind her head. His fingertips slid across one shoulder.

Her breathlessness returned, making her voice throatier than usual as she asked, "Ready for the movie?"

"In a minute. Let's talk awhile first."

Valerie was quick to agree. The night was a lovers' symphony of sighing wind and rain. It gave a heightened sense of warmth and closeness to the fragrant, softly lit atmosphere.

She wasn't aware of time's passage. Had someone asked her the hour, she wouldn't have known. She felt wonderfully relaxed sitting in the curl of his arm while they talked of everything and nothing at all.

With a little urging, she found out he liked country music and authentic New Orleans jazz.

The riotous burlesque of professional wrestling.

Football. Once upon a time, Friday nights had been reserved solely for the high-school games.

Show horses. He owned a few.

Her legs, which were a Thoroughbred's legs.

He did indeed read poetry, mostly when his mind was tired from making decisions. He also read World War II stories, and had a passion for Louis L'Amour's westerns. He'd collected every one the author had written.

He disliked pretentious people and mayonnaise. Sunsets made him feel melancholy; sunrises made him feel there was still hope. He played a mean game of golf and went fishing when the mood hit him. There were always fresh flowers in his house. He owned eighteen pairs of boots, ten Stetsons and slept in navy-blue silk pajamas ordered by the dozen from a Houston men's shop.

And he had to kiss her.

C.C. felt his words impact her. At some point he had managed to bring his hand close to her face without adverse reaction, and begun gently stroking her cheek and chin, just a brush of knuckles, back and forth, mesmerizingly. At least her dark eyes had become soft and velvety as she listened to his ramblings. He even felt beguiled himself with the murmurous weaving of voices.

She offered no resistance when, moving with care, he cupped the back of her head and touched his mouth to the fullness of hers. Lightly, lightly, restraining his urge to crush the berry-red lips as hunger surged up from dark depths, raw and passionately eager. He hadn't expected it, not this quickly. Not to this degree. With awesome control, he rubbed his mouth on hers, teasing, tempting, driving himself a little wild with the need to pull her into his arms and strain her into his body.

"Valerie..."

The sighing murmur of her name penetrated Valerie's rapidly scattering senses. Her body, which had become pliant, stiffened again, but only for a moment, only in the slow, caressing track of his hand down the back of her neck. It moved beneath her collar, each finger leaving a radiant streak of warmth in its wake. She turned, and curled her arms around his neck. The tension flowed out of her, starting with the lips she parted beneath his suddenly marauding mouth.

C.C. made a groaning sound at the sweet yielding. Control deserted him in the mindless pleasure of her response. He had to feel her body against his. With a lifting motion, he rose to his feet and drew her up with him. Eagerly she came into his embrace. Her head fell back and he ravaged her tender throat. Her tremulous breath stirred his hair as she surrendered to the compelling passion that caught them both unprepared for its savage demands. His breath was the whisper of her name ground into her lips by his hot, firm mouth.

Valerie trembled, her body growing correspondingly soft as his grew hard and taut, a demand in itself that she ached to answer. Some small portion of her mind was shocked at her intense response to his rugged sexiness. With an incoherent sound she pressed into him until a sheet of flame seemed to enclose them in a heated cocoon.

His mouth grew rough and urgent, and she answered with a surge of stunning desire. Over and over again he kissed her, taking her ever deeper into the swirling madness that enveloped her mind. Only when she heard a door close somewhere in the house was Valerie jolted to her senses.

Dimly, C.C. heard it, too. Summoning all his willpower, he dropped his arms and stepped away. The incandescent moment was past, she was through with it, and he wanted her outrageously.

"Sounds like Stephanie is home," Valerie said, striving for lightness. She felt as if she were coming up from some deep, dark well. She glanced at her watch. "Gracious, it's nearly eleven. We never did get to see that movie," she said brightly.

Hoping her smile would hold steady, she preceded him to the door. He still hadn't said anything, and that made her all the more nervous.

C.C. couldn't think of anything to say. His heart was still beating too hard to trust his voice. At the door, he put time and distance between them by reaching for his hat. Still shaken, and dead set against showing it, he leaned to her ear.

"See, told you I wasn't wrong," he murmured. Jamming on his Stetson, he strode out into the rain-swept night.

Five

Valerie waited until the sound of C.C.'s truck disappeared in a cloud of rain and mist before going to her bedroom. As if in a daze, she began to undress. Desire still throbbed through her body, and agitation shook the fingers that were trying to unhook her bra.

What happened to me? she wondered, dropping the garment on the dresser. How did I become so involved with a man so fast? A man I meant to keep at arm's length by claiming him as a friend.

And where had this intensity of need come from, welling up so rapidly she'd felt stunned with it?

Another question came hard and fast on the heels of that one as she straightened in front of her mirror. Why, all of a sudden, was she so vitally, painfully aware of her body? Over the past months she had developed a studied indifference to her appearance, never looking too closely at herself. But now she was looking, and the pain of actually *seeing* was suddenly as raw as the day they had removed the bandages.

The thought of C. C. Wyatt seeing her like this made her wince.

Hastily she pulled on a gown. She told herself that she was getting all worked up over nothing. No one had to see her like this; she had the controlling hand here. What she felt for C.C. was a simple case of not too surprisingly strong sexual attraction. He was a vibrant, virile male, and it had been a while, she reminded herself. A long while.

A frown lined her brow as she admitted to a fact less easily rationalized. In the past, she'd always been at ease with her sensual nature. But now she felt as ill equipped to deal with it as any pubescent female.

This was a source of embarrassment as well as anxiety, and she hated it. She had hated a lot of things lately, Valerie reflected moodily.

And as much as she disliked quarreling with her sister, she disliked even more the consequences of it. This was the second time in as many days that a compelling need for warmth and companionship had driven her to call C. C. Wyatt.

Saturday the weather turned almost balmy, and by Sunday, sunshine and ninety-degree temperatures had helped dry up the land. After arranging for the digging of his drainage ditches, C.C. drove over to his medical building.

He knew that Stephanie and her crew had been working all morning repairing their damaged landscape. But he didn't expect to find the two executive officers of Ander's Nursery and Landscape Design sitting on their bottoms spreading mulch. Both wore jeans and both, having gotten carried away with their work, were incredibly dirty.

C.C. felt a chauvinistic tug of anger. Irrationally, he felt it was all right for Stephanie to be mucking about in the dirt, but not Valerie.

Luckily he had the good sense to keep his thought to himself. Eyeing the two lovely, mud-daubed faces, he said, "I have an invite to that ritzy benefit party in Houston tonight, and I thought I'd ask you two. But a sight like this certainly gives a man pause. Our beloved Candace will be there, you can be sure of that," he added, naming an undauntable gossip columnist for a local newspaper.

"Who else is going to be there?" Stephanie asked shrewdly, sitting back on her haunches. He ticked off a few names.

"Nabobs all," she mused. "Count me in. Valerie?"

"Me, too," Valerie said without hesitation. She didn't enjoy this particular kind of social affair, but spending another evening with C.C. was too sweet a temptation to pass up. She frowned. "But this is rather short notice, C.C. I don't even have a dress to wear."

C.C. was too familiar with that feminine bit of reasoning to pay any attention to it. But admittedly it was short notice. Not only that, but it was an impulsive decision for him. He had intended skipping the boring affair. But an evening with Valerie could never be considered boring.

Before he could reply, Stephanie said, "You needn't go, Valerie, I'll do the honors for both of us."

"Thank you, Stephanie, but I'd like to go, and I brought along a 'little basic black,' so I guess I can make do," Valerie replied.

C.C.'s gaze sharpened at their cool, polite exchange. He had hoped they'd settled their differences by now, but apparently they hadn't. It rattled him. Needing a diversion, he looked around the long, curving lawn that flowed into beautifully landscaped beds and swept out in velvety green wings on either side of the broad building. The entrance, too, had been restored to its former splendor.

"Fine. Then I'll pick you both up at seven-thirty," he said brusquely. He stole another look at Valerie's unsettling face.

"You've done a good job here," he added, and left with a curt farewell nod.

He was still feeling jangled when he got home that evening. His stone-and-frame house, reminiscent of a Mediterranean villa he'd once visited and fallen in love with, featured a long, wraparound porch at the back. Tall red tilted shutters protected its glossy gray wood pillars and floors from sun and rain. Beds of lacy green ferns outlined the passage leading from the garage to white French doors that opened into the spacious den.

Mellow sunlight gilded its birch-paneled walls and imparted a pleasing glow to the wood floor of his study. After dropping off his briefcase, he went on to his bedroom.

It smelled of lemon oil and the coral roses his maid had arranged before she'd left. Tossing his hat on the crisp, geometric print bedspread that covered his big brass bed, he strode to the bathroom and flipped on the shower. Gray crystalline marble walled the cerulean-blue tub and shower areas. Handsome gold faucets and sleek, state-of-the-art fixtures gave it a richness that bespoke the rewards of success. A balm to a hard-working man who knew he'd earned it, C.C. thought as he stepped between the double jets of spray.

Distractedly he finished showering and toweled himself dry. His mind was still on the two women he'd just left. He knew that Stephanie had cause for her frosty reticence. She'd been hurt and embarrassed, the latter especially, since everyone on his jobs seemed to know the outcome of her love affair with Randy Bratton.

C.C. didn't like that, but there wasn't much he could do. Anything pertaining to Stephanie's love life provided titillating conversation for his construction hands. She flitted on and off their work scene like a bright and beautiful butterfly.

Their interest extended even to his own relationship with the attractive young woman, he remembered sourly, which annoyed him. She was young enough to be his daughter.

But his mind was thinking mainly about Valerie. Somehow, and rather mysteriously, he thought, the dissension between the two women had created within him a plaguing concern for her welfare.

Something else was giving him cause for concern. He doubted he'd be alone with her for a moment tonight, yet he was looking forward to the evening with fevered anticipation. Just being with her, talking with her, was sweetly satisfying.

And worrisome. Since meeting Valerie Hepburn, he hadn't so much as thought about any of the other women he knew, nor did he feel the slightest desire to see them.

C.C. grimaced. He knew how he affected her and found it immensely gratifying. But he didn't like her getting under *his* skin like this.

Setting her from mind with almost physical force, he concentrated on dressing. It surprised him sometimes that he felt as comfortable in formal wear as he did in jeans. An acquired talent, he mused, buttoning gold studs into his shirt front. He finished getting himself gussied up like some society swell, then surveyed his superbly tailored image. Unlike some Houstonians who wore boots with everything, he wore shining black shoes. But he sure did hate leaving his Stetson behind.

He was still thinking about Valerie when he drove through the soft autumn night. It even aggravated him that she had to settle for a "little basic black" for tonight, whatever that was. His mouth softened as he imagined her in the elegance of silk and fur and shining green stones.

Why green? She just looked like a lady who would like the green fire of emeralds, he answered himself somewhat irritably.

And Valerie in basic black, he discovered when she opened the door to him, was a sight for masculine eyes.

Her below-the-knee frock was cleverly fitted and draped by a master's hand. Her long, elegant legs were doubly sexy in black silk hose and high-heeled pumps. A jade necklace encircled her slender neck.

Not emeralds, but still green. A satin shawl poured down one shoulder like molten gold.

It was Stephanie's shawl; he'd seen it before. At least they were communicating a little, he thought with relief. He didn't notice what *she* was wearing at all.

A black velvet bow cradled Valerie's sleek French twist. Dark curls frosted her nape. C.C. had a disconcerting urge to kiss the tender spot. So he spoke heartily, complimenting both women on their appearance and ushering them out the door. Like some paid escort, eager to please, he thought dryly.

He was glad that Stephanie chose to sit in the back, giving Valerie the seat next to him. Her perfume misted his nostrils as he leaned over to fasten her seat belt. The dusky jasmine scent suited her perfectly tonight, at least in his opinion.

She didn't have much to say, leaving him and Stephanie to fill the conversational void. He didn't mind. She was beside him and, oddly enough, that was all that mattered right now.

But she did seem interested when Stephanie got him talking about his Hill Country ranch. So he elaborated each detail of his sun-bleached-stone and live-oak estate.

Valerie's rapt attention was genuine. C. C. Wyatt fascinated her. When she asked how he knew so much about the geology of his land, her reward was another nugget of information about him. Among many other things, he'd once been a young roughneck working on an oil rig, and had become friends with the company's geologist.

She withdrew again, picturing him as young and vulnerable. A roughneck. The term did not remotely fit the urbane man she watched from the corner of her eye.

Buffeted by disturbing emotions, she mentally tightened up as they entered the baroque ballroom of a downtown hotel. But she couldn't help responding to their glamorous surroundings. Banks of fragrant flowers and maidenhair ferns enchanted the senses. Expensive perfumes swirled around them like some exotic mist. Under the brilliance of an enormous crystal-and-gold chandelier, jewelry glittered with white, green, red and blue fire, and haute couture abounded.

Had not her frock come from a prestigious Parisian fashion house, she would have felt badly underdressed. As it was, she made her way through the crowd with languid ease, her head held regally high.

C.C. seemed well-known and liked. Introductions flew fast and furious and mostly over her head. To her astonishment, the newspaper columnist archly chided C.C. and Stephanie for withholding information from her, such as any future wedding plans. Gravely C.C. assured her she'd be the first to know should anything develop in that direction. To her chagrined relief, Valerie barely rated a curious glance from the woman.

Flashbulbs flashed. A surprisingly mediocre champagne made its rounds. She nibbled on pâté while covertly observing the focus of her inner attention. C.C. was warm, witty, delightfully charming with his extravagant drawl and vivid blue eyes twinkling through those impossible thickets of lashes. He radiated the strength and power of polished steel.

Such a desirable man, she mused, noting the feminine gazes that followed his broad-shouldered frame. I'm not the only one whose heart flutters when he comes near!

Stephanie, too, seemed at ease in her taxing environment. She wore a slim gown just one shade deeper than her eyes, and a rope of cultured pearls hung down her bare, golden back. Valerie took pride in her sister's beauty and poise. She held her own with the powerful men introduced to her by C.C.

Valerie's cosmopolitan decorum held steady until they left the ballroom and were waiting for their car to be brought around. Then she let herself relax. Her feet were bemoaning her choice of shoes, and it was blessed relief to slip them off in the shadowed car.

On the way home the conversation centered on the various people they'd met, particularly the professional contacts Stephanie had made. The business discussion enabled Valerie to lean her head back against the seat and indulge in girlish fantasy. She and C.C. were returning home from a date, and he would kiss her at the door...

He didn't, of course, not with Stephanie there with them. But Valerie had the delicious certainty that he wanted to. Thanking him for a pleasant evening, she bid him goodnight and followed her sister inside.

As she had done for the past few days, Stephanie said a short good-night and headed for her room.

"Stephanie, wait a minute. Let's talk, please?" she requested, catching her arm.

"Val, I don't want to talk. I'm tired and I want to go to bed. Good night," Stephanie said, and hurried on.

Her lovely mood shattered, Valerie veered toward her own bedroom. Her mind was churning and her eyes stung. Her heart ached. She missed her kids; she missed her own home. She wanted someone to hold her, to caress and soothe away the hurt. And she wanted that someone to be C.C. Wyatt.

She yearned for the good-night kiss she'd been denied, and an end to her fearful confusions. Most of all, she wanted an end to disharmony, and a return to her and Stephanie's lovely new friendship.

Well, she thought sadly, remembering her sister's hostility, these stimulating troubles would soon be over. She'd meant to stay another week regardless of her decision. But the situation between them was becoming too dispiriting to suffer any longer. They could conduct their future business by telephone.

And C. C. Wyatt would be gone from her life as easily as he came into it.

Maybe it was all just as well, she told herself stoutly. She was still worried about how her children would take such a move, and it wouldn't hurt to put some distance between herself and the man who was stealing ever deeper into her heart.

Giving into the misery of her sensible conclusion, she laid down on the bed and cried.

It seemed only a short time later that she awoke. But morning's pale, watery light was invading her windows. Drearily she realized it was raining again. Becoming aware of the warm weight beside her, she turned, and found Stephanie sitting on the edge of her bed.

Her breath caught as she looked up at the younger woman. "Stephanie? Are you all right, honey?"

Stephanie sighed and pushed at her tangled hair. "I'm all right. Or would be, if I wasn't such an idiot," she said wearily. "Val, I'm sorry. I didn't mean for you to get hurt, too, in this mess. I'm so ashamed of the way I've been acting. I've been hurting so and I guess I had to blame it on someone—anyone but myself. Oh, Val, I've been such a fool!" With her soft cry, she threw herself into Valerie's outstretched arms.

Valerie held her as she would one of her sobbing children, stroking, making little comforting noises. Gradually the heaving shoulders quietened.

"You okay now, Steffie?"

"Okay as I'll ever be, I guess."

"No, this will pass, you'll see, and you'll be the wiser for it. Do you want to talk about him?"

Stephanie violently shook her head. "I've wasted enough time on that—that wombat!"

Chuckling a little, Valerie handed her a tissue. Stephanie had a mist of freckles across the bridge of her nose and they seemed to pop out with her vehemence. "What do you want to do, then?"

"Kill him, I guess." Stephanie managed a weak smile. "But despite him needing it so much, I think that's still against the law."

"Well, law or no law, I'd love to get my hands on him right now," Valerie said grimly. "At the very least he would walk hunched over for a year or two!"

Her tone was fierce, her expression ferocious. Stephanie was astonished. "I didn't know you could be such a tigress, Val," she said faintly.

"I can when one of my own is hurt or threatened," Valerie replied darkly as she looked at her weeping sister.

"Well, I…well, thank you, I'm very glad I'm one of your own," Stephanie said with a tiny laugh. She sobered and mopped her wet face. "I'm also surprised that I am, after the way I've been acting. Val, be patient with me. I don't know how to handle heartbreak, not very well, anyway."

"Who does?" Valerie asked softly, shivering.

"Yeah, who does." With a noticeable effort, Stephanie squared her shoulders. "Valerie, have you made up your mind about moving yet? Despite my stupid behavior, I really want you here. I want us to be sisters. Sisters who can give each other a good shake when they need it," she ended with a wan attempt at humor.

Valerie bit her lip, suddenly swamped with a kind of dazzling joy composed of too many different elements to ever sort through. Last night's fear and misery suddenly seemed very far away. After all, the children were in boarding school; it wasn't as if they would be pulled away from their home and friends. And she'd developed a toughness that could handle C.C.

"And I want to be here. I want to start a whole new life," she said fiercely. "So, yes, you've got yourself a real sister, sister mine!"

The rain continued, but softer, creating an almost lulling effect as Valerie showered and dressed that evening. She and Stephanie had decided to have a little celebration of her decision to become a Texan.

"We'll invite a dozen people or so, some couples, some singles, a good mix," Stephanie enthused.

Watching her, Valerie had laughed aloud. Stephanie did love to party! She dressed and went to the kitchen to fix some snacks. The telephone rang. Valerie knew who it was before she picked up the receiver. C.C. Intuition seemed to reach out and span the distance between them until she could see in her mind's eye that it was he on the other end of the line.

Still, she wasn't prepared for the effect his deep voice had on her senses, nor for the disappointment that squeezed her heart as he regretfully declined her invitation to join them tonight. He had another engagement.

Valerie realized that she'd developed a rather strong proprietary air about him herself. Perhaps more than that. She felt a hot stab of something that could be called jealousy.

"What are you celebrating?" he asked.

"All in good time," she murmured.

"Hmm. I don't have to be at this other affair until eight-thirty. You think I could come by for an hour or so? I'd like to attend your celebration."

Annoyed that she was so relieved by his acceptance, she replied airly, "Why not? There's always room for one more. Seven-thirty. Sharp."

She heard his low rumble of laughter and her heart turned over. *Oh, Valerie, what are you getting yourself into?*

"Trouble," she muttered, hanging up. "And I can't wait for it to get here."

Despite her self-doubts, Valerie felt uncommonly good as the house began to fill up with people. There were three couples, and five single males of assorted ages and sizes with voices capable of shaking the rafters.

"You do seem to know an awful lot of men," she told Stephanie as they filled baskets with pretzels and chips.

"I work with a lot of men. Dave and John managed two of the job sites I worked on. They made it a lot easier for me to get in and out without running the gauntlet of 'Hey, baby.' Bob and I went to school together, and Dugan..." She nodded toward a tall, portly gentleman in dungarees and a plaid shirt. "I asked for you. He's a nice guy, Val. A little country, but still..."

"I don't mind country, Steffie. But I do mind triple chins and beer bellies. And if you don't stop trying to fix me up, I'm going to swat your fanny," Valerie threatened, her voice taking on a lilt as C.C. knocked on the screen door and then stepped inside.

His keen gaze swept over her plum-colored sweater and slacks, then up to her sister's face. "Why are you trying to fix Valerie up?" he growled, handing Stephanie his hat.

"That's what sisters *do,* C.C.," Stephanie quipped as she moved to the coatrack.

Valerie stood very straight as she looked at him. All he had done was glance at her and instantly the space between them was so taut with sensual tension that she felt suspended. He looked so wonderful, so alluring, she thought. Raindrops clung to his leather-covered shoulders and curled his dark gold hair. The glistening bead on one unruly side-burn begged to be brushed off by feminine fingers. Clasping hers, she smiled because she had no choice; his face was too pleasing.

She hung up his coat while Stephanie carried a tray of wineglasses into the spacious den where the party had congregated. When Valerie started to follow, he placed a restraining hand on her arm.

"You and Steph'nie friends again?" he asked, his gaze alert as she looked up at him.

"Yes, we've worked things out between us." His hand felt good on her arm.

"Is she okay?" C.C. gave her arm a little stroke.

"Of course she's okay—the man's a doughnut hole, C.C.," she said indignantly. Scowling at his rich chuckle, she suggested they join the rest of the guests at the table.

Valerie was pleased at how easily he fit into the lively group. During the festive hour that followed, she had to force herself to pay equal attention to the other men. Dugan really did seem to be a nice guy. But he couldn't compete with the man who sat across from her, watching her with those blue, blue eyes and a faintly crooked smile.

"I'd kind of like to know what we're celebrating," he said, accepting a glass of wine.

"We're celebrating Val's decision to pull up stakes and relocate here," Stephanie answered, lifting her glass. Her eyes still had that bruised look, but her smile was joyful.

With much ado, they toasted the decision. "I'm glad to hear you're staying, Valerie," Dugan said, low, but not low enough.

"So am I, Valerie," C.C. drawled, gazing at her over the rim of his glass. "Steph'nie needs someone to keep her in line!"

Everyone laughed. Valerie's gaze was still locked with C.C.'s, her shining brown eyes reflecting the gladness in his as they shared the moment. Fearing someone would notice the overlong glance, she averted her attention to her glass and its sparkling trail of bubbles.

"What will your kids say to this? Have you told them yet?" C.C. asked conversationally.

"No, not yet. This is too 'really, radical major,' to quote Brenda's favorite expression, to tell them over the telephone. I'll wait until I go home for Thanksgiving. But they're good kids, always quick to show their support and concern." Her mouth went awry. "Lately the girls have been on my case about getting out and finding myself a—" She stopped abruptly.

"A boyfriend," Stephanie finished for her, laughing as Valerie blushed.

"Well, they've just discovered boys," she explained with another wry smile.

"When are you moving here?" asked C.C. and another man simultaneously.

She answered the other man. "Not until after Christmas."

"Oh, but Val, that's over two months away," Stephanie protested.

"I know, but I want the children to spend Christmas in their own home." Valerie dared another glance at C.C.'s handsome face. "But I'll be around here for a while. With Nana and the children away at school, there's no one needing me at home. And I doubt that Robert's business partners will miss me all that much. In fact, they've been wanting to buy me out for some time now."

"Is it a good offer?" C.C. asked sharply.

"Why, yes, I think so," Valerie said, startled.

"Why don't you let me look at it before you accept?"

"Thanks, C.C., but my attorney will handle it," she replied, shying away from this too-personal offer.

He had to leave a short time later. Valerie walked him to the door and helped him on with his coat. She smiled as he threaded his fingers through his hair and followed it with the Stetson.

Taking advantage of their moment alone, C.C. touched the soft, loose hair gathered at her nape. "I'm glad you're staying, Valerie. We'd all miss your smile if you took it away."

"Thank you," Valerie murmured, flushed with sudden warmth. "I'm glad I'm staying, too. I'd forgotten how enjoyable it is to make new friends."

"Me, too," he said.

His hand slid beneath her hair. Her eyes opened wide and she drew an interrupted breath as he bent his head. His mustache brushed her lips, then tickled her nose as he set his mouth on hers with an alluringly soft touch. He held the kiss just for an instant, just long enough to send a fiery thrill sizzling through her veins before he slowly withdrew. Even then the clean, spicy scent of him drifted through his heathery linen shirt to tantalize her senses.

She wanted to throw herself into his arms and melt into his big warm male body. Breathless, tingling, she cleared her throat. "What was that for?"

Lazily he smiled. "Just a good-night kiss between friends."

"You know better," she rebuked.

"Oh, yes, I know better. I'm just making sure you do. Good night, Valerie." Tipping his hat, he opened the door.

Valerie closed it behind him, then placed its solid bulk against her back for a moment. Idly, intensely, she wondered about the woman who would share the remainder of his evening.

And his night?

Her mouth tightened as jealousy tossed another dart into soft, sensitive flesh. C. C. Wyatt, she admitted, was a dangerously exciting man, capable of supplanting a woman's common sense with witless emotions if she wasn't careful.

As she headed back to the den, she wondered, not for the first time tonight, if her decision to change her life was for the better, or for the worse.

Either way, she was going to find out. She was committed now.

Six

Awakening from a disturbing dream, Valerie flopped onto her stomach with a muttered oath. Last night she'd drank too much wine, gone to sleep filled with doubts and misgivings and awoke in the same condition plus a small headache.

It's all C.C.'s fault, she thought irritably. She wondered how he felt this morning, and if he was in bed alone. The jealousy that thought aroused irritated her even more. Stop it, Valerie, she admonished herself sternly. You have no claim on C. C. Wyatt, no right to resent him seeing other women.

That truth tasted like a green persimmon. Mouth drawn, she stopped before the mirror and stared at her image. A tiny, gentle smile softened her expression. In her flowered pajamas, with her hair in winsome disarray and her cheeks still flushed from sleep, she had a certain soft prettiness about her.

Sometimes, like now, she caught glimpses of that pleasing aura. But her altered perception of herself quickly interfered and her smile faded. Secretly she was appalled that the loss of a breast could create such a perceived deficiency in her body image. But it did, and she couldn't seem to change that.

Perhaps if she hadn't been left to cope alone with the aftereffects of breast cancer treatment, she would have a better self-image, Valerie reflected bleakly. But there had been no intimate relationship, no loving, supportive husband or lover to help restore her confidence in her physical attractiveness . . .

Self-pity was a rotten way to start a day. Shrugging, she put on a robe, sashed it tightly and strode to the empty kitchen.

A cup of coffee lifted her mood somewhat. The radiant autumn morning did the rest. Valerie's senses opened to the fullest as she absorbed the beauty of the day. The air was scented with the rosemary bush she brushed against, the sky was porcelain blue, the first sun rays warm on her face. Every leaf and blade of grass was bathed in silvered dew. It felt deliciously cold around her bare feet. Pausing beside a young dogwood tree, she sipped her coffee and mused over the especially vivid dream that had awakened her.

C.C. was in it, of course. C.C. seemed to be in most of her dreams lately, she conceded wryly. They'd been making love. Sweet, passionate, trouble-free love, the kind where clothes magically fall off and lights dim themselves and everything goes smooth as silk. As if it had actually happened, she remembered the feel of his mouth on hers, his big hands on her body, his expert caresses, the sheer loveliness of being filled with him . . .

Rosy-cheeked from her warm bath of thoughts, she looked up with an embarrassed little laugh as Stephanie stepped out on the porch. Valerie felt a stab of envy, then a searing rush of tenderness. Despite the perfection of womanly curves, her sister looked almost childlike with her sleepy green eyes and tousle of red-gold hair. Impulsively she ran across the grass and hugged the younger woman.

"You okay, darling?"

"Better. Battered, but better," Stephanie quipped gallantly.

Linking arms, they returned to the kitchen, chatting about the benefit they had attended with C.C. night before last. He and Stephanie were mentioned in the morning paper.

"We're referred to as 'that toothsome twosome,'" Stephanie said dryly. "Honestly, that woman! Where does she come up with things like that?"

"I think it's in their genes," Valerie said, chuckling. She refilled their coffee cups before asking the question that had been nagging her for the past two days. "Do people really think you and C.C. have something going? Something serious, I mean."

Stephanie shrugged. "He's gorgeous and single. It comes with the territory, I guess, even though it's not true. At any rate we both refuse to acknowledge gossip or dignify it with an answer."

Valerie's little shudder concealed her peculiar relief. "I'm glad it's you sharing that kind of limelight. I don't think I could handle it. Would you like bagels and cream cheese for breakfast? I'll fix it. I'll also share those letters on the counter with you if you'd like. They're from the children. Brenda's in love with the gardener, it seems," she chattered on. Last night's misgivings had faded in the pleasure of beginning the day like this.

Excitement joined her good feelings as Stephanie, taking up the letters, said distractedly, "C.C. wants our bid for that apartment complex on Taylor Road this morning, but I've got appointments until two. First one's a dental checkup," she explained, making a face. "Which means you'll also have to open up for me this morning. Would you mind taking it to him? He'll be out at the Parade of Homes site until noon."

"I'd be glad to," Valerie replied. She wanted very much to be a useful part of the nursery staff. If that meant running errands, then so be it, she told herself, sternly disregarding her tremulous pulses. Seeing C.C. again was just an extra little bonus.

At eight-thirty she opened the nursery and greeted the small staff as they arrived. There were three large trees to be delivered and planted before the men left for the new job her sister had contracted the week before. That they accepted Valerie's authority without question was sweetly satisfying.

At ten she placed the necessary papers in her brown leather satchel and got into her car. She hummed as she entered the broad parkway that led into a heavily forested little town. She ought to be pondering the things that had worried her last night, the move and its effect on the children, the stress of making a whole new life for them and for herself.

And C.C., of course. Always C.C., she thought with an itchy little shiver. But it was a fine autumn day and she was going to meet a vital, attractive man. It was hard to think sobering thoughts when her spirits were flying like kites before a high wind.

There were several men at the site, but it was easy enough to pick out C.C. with his sun-colored hair and that lean physique clad in wonderfully fitting slacks and a knit shirt. He stood tall and straight and light on his feet, a weightless stance. A silver-buckled belt defined his trim waist. The Stetson he wore shoved back on his head was so weathered it was no longer true black.

A smile curved his mouth when he saw her, and his mustache moved with it, enticingly. She couldn't help smiling in return. Her stomach lurched as she noted the curiosity in the other men's eyes. She didn't want to be the subject of speculation! Head held high, she picked her way over the roughly cleared ground, glad that she'd worn flat-heeled shoes.

As she met their appraising gazes, Valerie was also glad she'd chosen a tailored green jacket and slacks for her workday attire. She faintly inclined her head before turning her eyes on C.C.

"Excuse me, gentlemen," C.C. said, and walked to meet her.

"Good morning, Valerie."

His deep voice seemed to slide along her skin like rough velvet. She cleared her throat and returned his greeting.

When he introduced her to the other men, she offered her hand in a firm, businesslike handshake. Then she withdrew the papers from her bag and gave them to C.C.

He stuck them in his shirt pocket. "Oh, I've got a check for you in my truck," he said. "It's for the job you just finished." He steered her toward the vehicle with a hand under her arm.

Warmth radiated from each finger and streaked down her skin. "Did you have a good time last night?" she asked abruptly. "After you left the house, I mean."

"No."

She stopped just as abruptly, luckily beside the truck.

"No?"

"No." Leaning against the door, C.C. studied the papers she'd given him. "I kept wishing I was with you," he replied absently.

She stared at him, at the sun-streaked hair falling over one side of his forehead, at the shadow of lashes on his cheeks. Having gotten exactly the answer she wanted, she didn't know what to do with it.

Reaching through the truck's open window, he grabbed a large checkbook and detached the prepared check. Their fingers touched as she took it and a sweet fire raced along her skin.

"Thank you," she still had wits enough to say. He smelled wonderful. She was suddenly very hungry. Remnants of her early-morning dream kept floating around her mind.

"You're welcome," C.C. replied, still distracted. His mind had veered to the woman he had dined with last night. Dating another woman had been a rather desperate attempt to slow his snowballing interest in Valerie Hepburn. The evening had been a dud. He'd been bored and curiously hungry for something besides food or sex, neither of which he'd wanted last night.

He wanted this woman, wanted her so much it was a tight ache low inside him. A sexual want, he told himself. Nothing deeper than that.

Replacing the checkbook, he allowed his gaze to rest on her flushed face. Such soft, beautiful skin. He longed to touch, to see if that softness held true all over. Instead he asked, "Listen, would you like to take a little ride? I have something to show you. A surprise."

"What?"

"If I told you, it wouldn't be a surprise. You can follow me in your car if you want," he said, acknowledging the hint of coolness in her manner.

"All right. Where is it?" Valerie asked, intrigued despite herself.

"Meet me at that little store where we had soft drinks that day. The one with the lake. You remember where it is?"

Valerie nodded.

"Let me get through with these characters and I'll join you there, all right? I'll be about ten minutes."

"Fine," she said. Her heart was beating absurdly fast as she left him. Guiltily she remembered she'd forgotten all about the bid she'd just given him. She should be anxious about it, for it was a good-sized job and she was in the business now. But, foolishly, all she could think of was what he'd said. *I kept wishing I was with you.*

When he arrived at the store, she was waiting out back under the willow tree.

"This way," he said, taking her hand. They walked in silence down the dirt path to the opposite side of the lake where another enormous willow sheltered a tiny table and carved log benches. It was a wonderfully private place, but Valerie was puzzled since they hadn't bought food or drink.

Her puzzlement ended as he guided her through a fringe of young trees to a small pond, not much larger than a children's wading pool. Here, amidst reeds and lily pads, a mother duck and six tiny yellow-and-black ducklings floated on the dappled water.

"Oh, C.C., they're lovely!" she exclaimed delightedly. She knelt beside the bank, laughing as the mother duck promptly steered her brood to the opposite side. "But how did you know they were here?"

"They nest here every year about this time," he said, his voice gruff response to her pretty pleasure. He helped her up, his big hand enveloping hers entirely. "Shall we sit down? We can see them from here."

She nodded, her throat tight from his delicious nearness. Sitting down on the satin-smooth benches, they watched the ducklings for a while. She could think of nothing to say.

Apparently neither could he.

"I could tell you a story," she offered as the silence stretched out between them.

He looked startled. "A story?"

"Um-hum. I'm very good at storytelling. I had a lot of practice with the children, you see. Have you heard the one about the princess who was so tiny she bathed in a dewdrop?"

Relaxing, he chuckled and propped his chin in his hand. "What about her?"

"As you might expect, she lived a very precarious life."

He burst out laughing. Valerie's own laughter welled up in soft counterpoint. He was relaxed, at ease. Daringly she said, "Now you tell me a story. About why you and Jordan aren't close."

He eyed her. "Why are you so hung up on that?"

"I'm not 'hung up' on that," she reproved. "I'm just interested. I've got children, too, and it saddens me to think what you've missed. And are still missing, for that matter. I don't know how I'd get along without my family." She caught back the russet locks escaping from the malachite barrette restraining her hair. "You must have been very young when Jordan was born. Almost a boy yourself."

Her eyes were soft, her tone inviting. C.C. found himself taking the bait with ridiculous ease.

"Not quite eighteen," he said. "I was working on a ranch at the time, one of those big showplaces: Thoroughbred horses, some rare longhorn cattle. She was the owner's daughter, just turned eighteen, the apple of her daddy's eye, used to getting what she wanted."

"And she wanted you," Valerie put in, statement, not question.

"Yeah, she did." His mouth twisted. "At any rate, we started fooling around, and we got caught. I was agreeable to making it right, but she was appalled at the thought of marriage. Little rich girls might play around with the hired hands, but they didn't marry them. But back then no little rich girl had a baby out of wedlock, either, no decent one, anyway. Her father laid down the law and we obeyed it. We got married."

Valerie sighed. "I can imagine what kind of marriage it was. Did you love her?"

"No. Just temporarily enthralled by what she symbolized to a tenant farmer's son." He laughed through his nose, a mocking sound. "Dazzled, not in love, a fact she never forgave me for. But you're either in love or you're not, you can't make it happen. And it wasn't much of a marriage. Right after the baby was born, she filed for divorce, which, with her father's help, went through like a breeze. Then he whisked them off to England, to his wife's aunt."

"You didn't get custody rights?"

"I had no rights."

"Oh, nonsense, of course you had rights," she asserted angrily. A man's desire to love and care for his children was very important to her. "Surely you didn't let them get away with it?"

C.C. didn't like where this was going, but he felt oddly helpless to stop it. "Valerie, I wasn't given much choice in the matter. I was a drifter without a family. My mother had died by then, and all I had left were a few obscure relatives. I was certainly not a fit daddy for Jordan Pierce Wyatt. Look, let's just drop it, shall we? I don't know why I'm trying to explain it, anyway."

"Because I want to understand, that's why," she said, her voice softening. Her head tilted slightly. "And because you want me to understand."

She sure had *that* right, thought C.C., admitting his sudden raw need to regain her good impression of him.

"Valerie, I was just eighteen at the time of the divorce, not exactly King Solomon. I didn't know what to do. So I did nothing. Afterward I joined the service—"

"You were in the service? In Vietnam?"

"Yeah. I was in Vietnam for an eighteen-month tour of duty. Seventeen months into my hitch I took some shrapnel, not enough to kill me, but enough to get me home, and believe me, I was ready to go home. I bummed around for a while after that, taking whatever job was available:

roughneck, cowboy, carpenter. The latter is what got me
started in this business. I loved it, and I was lucky enough
to apprentice to one of the best. He's the one who got me
interested in architecture, and then night school. Well, anyway, when Jordan was nearly five, she brought him back
from England, and I had him for a few weekends before she
returned to Europe. I tried legal proceedings to keep him,
but..."

C.C. rubbed his brow. "Maybe you truly can't fight the
system, I don't know. Or maybe I just didn't try all that
hard. I'd already met Hope by then. We fell in love, got
married, had a kid right off the bat..." He shook his tawny
head. "Everything I wanted so much, right there in my
hands. So I just...gave up on Jordan, I guess. I'm ashamed
to say that he took a back seat to my new family, but he did.
And he knows it. He knew I didn't need him then. So now
he doesn't need me. Turnabout, fair play. Only I *do* need
him."

Looking chagrined at having exposed his deepest emotions, to a woman whose opinion shouldn't matter so much
but did, he went on briskly, "Well, that's the story you
wanted. Did you like it?"

"No, I hated it." Valerie bit her lip. She didn't want to
find a flaw in his character. Still, she wouldn't want a perfect man, she argued with herself. Perfection in a person
would be intimidating, to say the least.

"C.C., it isn't entirely your fault that you and Jordan are
estranged," she said thoughtfully.

C.C.'s hand trembled ever so slightly as relief coursed
through him. "No? Whose, then?" he asked like a taunt.

"Let's just be kind and blame it on circumstances," Valerie replied on a softening note. C.C. wasn't making ex-
cuses for his actions. He had made mistakes, and he was
paying for them. Remembering that he had buried both a

beloved wife and a child during his lifetime, she touched his arm. "Thank you for sharing that confidence with me."

Without speaking, C.C. squeezed the hand resting so lightly on his arm. His relief swiftly changed to something much more potent as he glanced at her. The freshening wind played in her hair and cupped the shadow-striped fabric of her blouse around her breasts, much as his hands ached to do. He met her luminous dark gaze and had to look away lest she see the hunger in his.

"You're welcome, I suppose." He grunted. His lashes slowly fanned up to reveal blue eyes lit with a spark of humor, and something else. "Even if you do strip away my privacy and flay me with it."

"I'm sorry," she said demurely.

"Now why don't I believe that?" he wondered aloud, and her laughter came softly. It stilled as he leaned forward and slowly slid a hand up her neck and along her jaw.

"Go to a concert with me tonight?" he murmured.

"No, I don't think so, I—C.C., please," she said huskily, fighting her weakness for him. Her eyes widened and locked with his as he cradled the tender curve of her cheek and held his hand there. The atmosphere between them changed so swiftly she shivered.

"Such a delicate face," came his half whisper. "So fragile. Do you know what a delicate face you have? Makes a man want to go slay a dragon or two...or at least an alligator." The humor left his eyes, replaced by an odd intensity. His thumb rolled on a cushion of warmth down her neck and back up again. "Soft skin, so warm and smooth. Like satin..."

"C.C.," Valerie warned, struggling to resist his airy assault on her senses. She stilled again as he spread his fingers to encompass her mouth, tracing the shape of her lips before he brushed them with his, maddeningly light, a velvet whisk of sensation. The tip of his tongue slid in ever so briefly, then withdrew to trace the outline of her lips.

His mouth touched hers again. Desire flared like physical fire. It snatched at her breath and thickened his murmurous voice. They were totally alone at this end of the lake, and the shadowed bower in which they sat enhanced the romantic moment.

His mouth pressed harder. She could not steady her tremulous voice. "C.C., don't."

"No one can see us," he murmured on her lips.

"I know." She turned her face slightly and drew a breath. "But that's not my problem."

His forehead touched hers. "What is your problem? Tonight's concert?" he asked, though he knew full well what the problem was—at least, what his was: this minor bit of love play was arousing explosive feelings. He wanted to make love to her, right here, on the table, the grass—he didn't care where, just as long as they were together. I didn't know you were so desperate, Wyatt! he jabbed at his blazing need.

He heard her draw another, deeper breath before moving her face aside. "No, it's not that. It's what comes afterward."

"Breakfast?"

"C.C., will you stop it?" she asked, both delighted and exasperated at once.

"Sorry." His mustache quirked, affirming his lie. He dropped his hand. "About tonight..."

She began nervously clearing the table. "C.C., slow down, hmm? I like to kiss you. But I'm not ready to go beyond kissing."

Something shadowed her eyes, something that gentled his heart. He wished he had a cigarette to light up and fill the next few seconds. But he'd quit smoking years ago.

"I think you are." His mustache quirked again. "But I'll try to restrain myself, Valerie."

Valerie let out her breath. "I thank you," she replied dryly.

With precise, spare gestures, she stood and smoothed her hair. There was an elegance even in the movements of her hands, C.C. thought. He smiled, and she arched an eyebrow in question.

"You're one classy lady, Ms. Hepburn," C.C. said with a trace of huskiness. "It's going to be a pleasure getting to know you better. A rare and wonderful pleasure."

Her distracted state of mind did not escape Stephanie's notice. "Well, hello! Where have you been? With C.C.?" she asked as Valerie entered the office later that afternoon.

"Yes. He took me to see some newborn ducklings, then we talked awhile," Valerie said ever so casually. "How did your dental checkup go?"

"Look, Ma, no cavities." Thoughtful green eyes followed Valerie's pacing figure. "Should I start including C.C. in my matchmaking efforts?"

Brought up short, Valerie said crisply, "Don't be ridiculous, Stephanie."

"Well, it appears to me that you two are together a lot," Stephanie protested her judgment. "I mean, Val, baby ducklings? And then a long talk?" she teased.

"C.C. has his troubles just like any other man and he seems to feel that I'm safe to confide in," Valerie replied with exaggerated dignity. Exasperation tinged her voice as her sister snorted disbelief. "Steffie, wasn't it you who said that C.C. could have his choice of young, beautiful, unencumbered women, none of which, I might point out, describes me? I'm not beautiful, I'm nearly middle-aged and I'm very much encumbered, and I'm not even a complete woman. So let's table the subject, shall we?'' she suggested. Her voice was too sharp. But the truth stung.

"Well, all right," Stephanie sniffed. "Personally I think you're a damn attractive lady and I don't see how you can feel like less than a complete woman. And although I could point out that you're not quite a toothless old crone yet, I won't bother you with useless information."

Valerie accepted her insecurities with a humorous grunt. "Thank you. Now if you don't need me any more today, I'd like to go to the bookstore. I want to pick up a few books to add to the ones you already have at home. Mostly plant books—I don't think I'll ever be any good at landscape design. But I want to contribute something to this business, Steffie," she said earnestly. "Something besides just being here, or running errands, although I don't mind that—" She stopped, catching her sister's quick, sly smile.

Scowling, Valerie grabbed her bag off the desk. "Here's the check for the job we just finished for C.C. Now if you'll excuse me..." Head high and cheeks burning, she walked back out to her car.

During the next two weeks, C.C. popped into and out of Valerie's life like a stimulating turbulence that affected every part of her being. Logic's arguments to the contrary, she was always glad to see him, a blitz of gladness that streaked running fire through her veins each time he came close enough to see, to smell and, especially, to touch.

She was both perturbed and thrilled to realize that, for the first time in years, she felt wonderfully lighthearted and gay, eager to face most of her challenges. She felt almost reckless at times, a throwback to her younger years when she'd taken on Europe and a new husband with audacious daring.

Yet there were times in C.C.'s presence when she was struck with an almost scalding awareness of her body. Her reaction was automatic: an elusive withdrawal that unknowingly enriched C. C. Wyatt's inner restlessness.

He felt different since his highly personal talk with her. Different how, he couldn't readily say, but a burden had been lifted from him, a load of guilt that he'd carried all these years. Hearing himself explain it, in hard, spoken words, had cleared up some of the contempt in which he held himself where Jordan was concerned. Not all of it, for he'd been really piling it on in the past few years. But enough to leave room for compassion for the young, confused man C. C. Wyatt had once been.

And still was, he acknowledged wryly. Still confused and, in his secret heart, still young and vulnerable. If he wasn't, he would never have succumbed to a soft, maternally sweet voice inviting him to unburden himself.

He wanted to be with her because being with her made him feel absurdly good. But she refused his social invitations with the excuse of work. She was trying to integrate herself into Stephanie's game plan for the future, she explained gravely.

His pride smarting, he decided to back off. But working together as they did brought him back into Valerie's disturbing presence again and again. Well, he couldn't help that, C.C. defended. Business was business.

One evening he drove Stephanie home from his job site when her truck refused to start. "I'll get a mechanic out there in the morning," he told her.

"You don't need to do that, C.C., we'll take care of it," Valerie said, stepping outside. "Now that you're here, though, stay and have a bite with us," she invited so sweetly he was instantly furious. "It's just chili and crackers, but there's only Steffie and me, and we're setting up a table in the living room by the fire."

"Thanks, but I have another engagement tonight," he said stiffly, the truth, though by now he was regretting it.

"Oh. Well, another time, then," she replied lightly. "Bye, C.C. Drive carefully," she advised.

"I will. Good night, Valerie," he said, smiling.

C.C. clenched the hands that wanted to shake her and left the warm, bright house for his own dark abode.

Seven

The following week was chilly and drab. Then November did one of its delightful about-faces and opened up like a yellow rose, full of warmth and sunshine and the icy fragrance of early-blooming camellias. But Valerie still felt the chill inside. It had been seven long days since C.C.'s presence had graced Stephanie's house.

Valerie couldn't help wondering if his absence had anything to do with her refusal to see him under more intimate circumstances. He did have a well-developed ego, she thought, careful not to give it more significance than was merited. She knew he was dating another woman; she'd glimpsed him and an attractive redhead entering the parking lot of a restaurant she and Stephanie were leaving. At least the redhead wasn't young enough to be his daughter, Valerie thought tartly.

She also wondered if her refusals to date him were motivated in part by the spasms of jealousy C.C.'s active social life aroused deep inside her, out of range of logic's influence. Obstinately she denied it—she had no cause to care what C. C. Wyatt did, or with whom.

During this past week she had established a routine that practically shouted her lack of need for C.C.'s presence. She got up with Stephanie and went to work from eight-thirty to six o'clock. Then they came home to eat leftovers or pizza or takeout Chinese. Sometimes Stephanie went out for a while; Valerie studied her many books or watched television, called her children, took a long, luxurious bath, went to bed. Thoughts of C.C. were most forcefully kept to idle speculation, which she only permitted for a moment or two.

Still, it seemed joyously right and fitting when he dropped by the nursery on this bright, balmy day to suggest she take the afternoon off for an expedition to a local art museum. A Georgia O'Keeffe exhibition, he added as further inducement.

Valerie bit her lip. The artist was one of her favorites. "Of course I'd love to see the exhibition. But we're pretty busy, C.C.," she said, determined not to betray how very much she wanted to go with him. "Let me speak to Stephanie about it."

Stephanie was all for it. She could handle things here.

That being decisively settled, Valerie rejoined C.C. in the fragrant little showroom. They walked outside, where flats of blossoming winter flowers created a miniature fairyland. "You really are busy," he said, looking around.

"A day like this brings out the gardeners in droves, it's like a fever in the blood, thank God!" she replied, gazing at the gratifying crowd of potential customers. "C.C., I need to stop at the house and put on a dress, this is far too casual," she said, fingering her slacks.

"You look fine to me," he said with a smile that curled her toes.

"Well, even so, I'd still like to change," she returned coolly. His smile faded a little and that pinched. She touched his hand. "You don't mind, do you?"

Gold sparks smoldered in his eyes as he caught her gaze. "I don't mind. It's much more private there than here."

"I don't know that we need privacy, but..." She shrugged. "I'll meet you at the house."

C.C. was waiting on the porch when she got home. When their eyes met, a faint, intimate smile curved his mouth. Watching him come toward her, tall and golden in the sunlight, Valerie had cause to question her lofty sentiments concerning platonic friendships between members of the opposite sex. The warmth gathering low in her stomach was not engendered by friendship.

"Hi again, C.C.," she said lightly. "I won't be but a minute. I don't have a key to the front door, just the back. You can wait in the solarium if you'd like?"

"I'd like." Taking her hand, he walked with her to the gate that led to the backyard.

She liked his clasp, liked the way hard, strong fingers gentled around hers. Her mood heightened dangerously. The day was so lovely. A breeze had come up and suddenly it was raining leaves, streams of them, red and brown and gold forming a carpet underfoot. Autumn, already touched by a soft frost, smelled wonderfully dark and earthy. C.C.'s scent blended with it to form a rare and sensuous perfume.

A little pulse beat swiftly at the base of her throat as she opened the door and they stepped inside the shadowed room. "How about a glass of wine while you wait?" she invited, gesturing toward the decanter and glasses that sat on a little portable bar. She poured two glasses, handed him one and took the other to her bedroom.

Valerie sipped the rich red wine as she dressed in a simple white silk blouse and a slim, dark green skirt. She added black pumps and gold hoop earrings, then brushed out her hair. It had grown back in swiftly after chemotherapy, softer and with a bit more auburn tint, she thought. A folded square of lilac, pink and gray silk, restrained the shining mass. After looping the sleeves of a rose-hued sweater around her neck, she walked back to the solarium.

It's just an afternoon at the museum, she reminded herself, striving to settle her fluttery nerves. But that quick, hot delight still danced in her blood as he came to meet her. "You look lovely," he said. Before she could thank him, he cupped the back of her head and kissed her, briefly, but not brief enough to escape the swift claws of desire.

Catching her breath, she drew back. "C.C., why do you do that, just grab me and kiss me like that?" she asked.

"I don't know. An urge just seems to come over me," C.C. said with a touch of acerbity. Hell, how did he know why he kissed her like that? He just wanted to, that's all.

"I suppose your other women friends like it, but—"

"My other 'women friends' don't get grabbed and kissed."

"They don't?" Valerie said, pleasantly startled. "Then why do I?"

"Believe me, if I knew I'd tell you, Val," C.C. said, using the diminutive for the first time. His voice lowered to huskiness as he slid his fingers gently through her hair and drew her unresisting face to his again. "You don't like it?" he asked, looking into her eyes.

"It's not that I don't like it, it's just . . ." She faltered as his breath brushed her cheek.

"Just?" he murmured, placing a tiny kiss on each corner of her lips.

"Just don't like to be taken by surprise . . . oh!" She gasped as his mouth set full on hers.

C.C.'s intake of breath echoed hers as he kissed her. When her lips parted beneath his, that electric shock of desire came again. He could taste the tang of wine, and something else, something vibrantly sweet and seductive. Her. The essence of Valerie, coming swift on his tongue as he explored her mouth.

He forgot they were leaving, forgot everything but the soft, delicious lips yielding to his hungered taking and giving of pleasure. Their bodies strained toward each other, wanting to touch, aching to touch. But although she was responsive, that elusive quality about her kept him from reaching out to take this pleasure, too. It was such a privilege just to do this.

She slipped her hands to his cheeks and kissed him with potent new urgency. With a heady little shiver, she accepted his tongue and drew in his breath. Her own sweet breath entered him and brought him swiftly to arousal. He traced her upper lip with the tip of his tongue, swept his mouth along the rich fullness of her bottom lip and back again to the swollen, peaked center.

They kissed for hours. Hours, she insisted dazedly, though only minutes passed. But a sensuous haze enveloped them, and his mouth—now rough, now gentle, warm and slow, then hot and greedy—was incredibly alluring. She couldn't get enough of it.

He was astonished at how satisfying this kind of kissing was. It filled up empty hollows deep within him and he wanted desperately to lie with her. Yet despite the burn of desire in his loins, he felt wonderfully warm and replete.

She could have gone on with this dark magic forever.

He wanted it never to stop.

Eventually she pulled away. His deep, steadying breath echoed hers.

He leaned his forehead against hers. "God," he whispered. "I don't know what it is you do to me, but I could crawl into the back seat of my old Buick and kiss you like this for a week. And I haven't owned an old Buick since I was eighteen. So what do we make of that?"

He sat back, eyes glinting. "What do we make of this relationship, for that matter?"

"I..." She licked her lips. "Nothing," she said with a hint of stubborn defiance.

"Not as long as you keep hiding from it, no," he responded dryly.

"I'm not hiding. I'm just being cautious. I'm careful about starting new relationships, because..." Valerie paused, torn. But to baldly tell him why, here in the bright light of day, was just too much for her. So she let the opportunity slip by. "Because I don't like to court trouble." Her eyes crinkled. "And you are trouble, C.C."

"Am I!" he said, liking that. It beat wondering if he'd had as much effect on her as he'd thought.

"Yes, you are," she affirmed, her mouth twisting. "Luckily I've reached the age of realizing that self-denial won't kill me. I'd think that you would have realized that by now, too."

His eyes flinted. "I practiced self-denial for two years after Hope's death. Then I realized that *I* was still alive and had to start living again instead of just functioning. Have you realized that yet, Valerie?" he asked very softly.

"Yes, of course I have. I worked through my grief and loss, just as you did," she replied, feeling defensive against those penetrating blue eyes. Hating the sliver of doubt that pierced her, she lifted her chin. "I'm a well-adjusted woman, C.C. Who does not, I might add, have to explain myself to you, or anyone else. Now if you don't mind, I'd like to change the subject."

"Touched a nerve, did I?"

"No." She sighed and looked away. "C.C., I really don't enjoy being analyzed."

C.C. picked up his glass and sipped his wine, studying her over its rim. There were secrets in the velvety brown eyes that flickered to his and then away. An enigma, he thought.

A delectable one, though. She was lovely in his eyes. Thirty-nine years of living had left its passage on her face, but the soft white blouse and open collar, the hair spilling around her shoulders, made her look like a schoolgirl. His throat tightened with tenderness. He cleared it.

"Sorry, I didn't mean to pry. It's just that you baffle me so. I think we've got a lot of things to learn about each other." He gave her a crinkly-eyed grin. "Do you want to start tonight?"

Oh, C.C.! "You just don't give up, do you!"

"Not easily, no." Sky-blue eyes locked with hers. "Do you want me to?"

Caught fair and square, she placed fingertips at her temples and massaged. "I don't know. You baffle me, too, C.C. Anyway, Stephanie and I are going to the movies tonight. We both adore movies. So I need to be home by six o'clock. Thanks for asking, though."

"Oh, you're welcome," C.C. said, sardonic. "At least I'm becoming inured to rejection."

Later that evening, sitting in a darkened theater, Valerie felt too fidgety to enjoy the film she and Stephanie were watching. Her mind kept going back to C.C., and the lovely interlude at the museum. It had been an entertaining, light-hearted, singularly satisfying togetherness. By the time they arrived back home, she was wishing she hadn't promised her evening to Stephanie.

On a more serious level, she kept recalling C.C.'s astute comments before they'd left for the museum. He had indeed hit a nerve when he'd questioned her adjustment to life without her mate. Could part of her reluctance to become romantically involved be due to that? Was she using her persistent sense of loss to block his advances? She didn't think so. What stopped her was the simple fear of being hurt.

She had been, once, prior to her surgery, when she'd lowered her guard to a handsome, likable man she'd met at a party. When her cancer had been discovered, he had been very supportive of her and had accompanied her to the hospital beforehand to view the videos that illustrated clearly what she could expect before, during and after surgery. Then he had broken off the relationship, explaining that he'd realized that he just couldn't deal with her affliction, and that her mastectomy turned him off physically.

His rejection stabbed her with pain. It stung pride and femininity alike. What do you care? she had admonished her wretched self. He doesn't mean anything to you, not really. Besides, you've already had love and marriage and children—the whole beautiful bit. It's not as if you need a man in your life.

She had convinced herself of that. Nonetheless, his words had stayed with her, like an oil slick at the back of her mind.

The following evening Valerie went out with Dugan. He was a pleasant enough escort, but she was bored and uncomfortable and regretted her acceptance. As gently as possible, she turned down another date.

C.C. and two other friends came to dinner the next evening. A blue norther had come roaring in that afternoon and dropped the temperature thirty degrees in an hour's time. By six o'clock it was cold and windy, and Valerie made comfort food: mashed potatoes, pork chops and baked squash, with banana pudding for dessert. Watching people enjoy the meal she had prepared was always a pleasure. Especially when one of those people was C.C., she admitted wryly.

She did not allow herself to be alone with him. After he left, she went to her bedroom and turned on the night lamp. Curling up on the window seat, just a windowpane away from the black, wet night, put her in a reflective mood. She thought back on her life, rambling through years of memories both happy and sad. She thought of Robert's death, and the seeming finality of the sexual part of her life. Then she thought of C.C. and the joyous urgency he could arouse within her with just a smile, a touch.

Shying away from that subject, she considered his relationship with Jordan and recalled the privilege of sharing C.C.'s sorrow. She had been awfully quick to absolve him of guilt in the matter. Logic of the brain? Or the heart?

Since she couldn't answer that, she got up to do some hand laundry, gathering up her three prosthetic bras and washing them in a mild soap solution. Maybe she'd absolved him too quickly, she mused. After all, if he wasn't a good father to his own child, it wasn't likely that he'd be any good with hers. She stilled, startled by her thought. She didn't know where it came from, nor did she care to acknowledge its implications.

She hung the garments over the shower rod to dry and went to bed in a somber mood.

Two nights later she sat in the den drinking port and reading a plant book. "So much to learn," she said to Stephanie, who was curled up in an armchair watching television and eating mandarin oranges straight from the can.

"You'll learn it," Stephanie assured her. "One thing to remember is that Houston's in zone eight—" She stopped as the telephone rang.

"It's probably for you," Valerie murmured.

Agreeing, for she had become very popular once it was known that she was a free agent again, Stephanie hurried to answer it.

"That was C.C.," she said when she returned. "He asked us to the shindig he's throwing Saturday night. I said we'd go. Well, that *I* would go. I didn't know about you. I think I'll ask Bobby, too, then he can drive us. You game?"

"I don't know," Valerie said with an inward sigh for her sudden race of pulse. She was trying to get a grip on herself where he was concerned. But mention his name and I start to salivate, she thought dryly.

"Oh, come on, you know you're dying to go," Stephanie teased. "What's it been now, three whole days since you've seen him?"

"Stephanie, that's enough. I don't like joking about a romance between C.C. and me," Valerie returned evenly. "I'm a little sensitive in that area, okay?"

"Why? Because you've lost a breast? Val, it doesn't matter—"

"It *does* matter—it matters a lot!" Startled by her vehemence, Valerie moderated her voice. "I'm sorry I snapped at you, but it does matter."

"I'm sorry, I didn't mean to sound callous, I just..." Stephanie shook her head. "But who am I to say how you should feel about it? I'm sorry, honey. I just thought it would be great if you two hit it off. And the party's a painless way to meet some more of our business associates," she added, her face lightening with relief at having found a neutral subject. "Bert Fuller's going to be there, and he's doing a lot of building out on Lake Conroe. Remember, Val, personal contact never hurts."

"All right, put that way, I'll go," Valerie replied, then had to laugh at her sham. She *was* dying to see C.C. again.

Besides, she was eager to see his house. A man's personal quarters revealed a lot about his character, she thought.

"It's dressy-casual," Stephanie said, bringing her to the subject of what to wear.

It was oddly important to Valerie that she look just right. Not young, nor even a hint of trying to be. No, poised, self-assured, with that touch of insouciance that casual elegance always lent her.

Unfortunately she had nothing in her closet that fit that description. So the next afternoon, she and Stephanie stole a couple of hours from work to go shopping.

Walking around the mall together, shopping, laughing, trying on and discarding clothes with giddy abandon, was an enjoyable new experience for them both. They were becoming more like true sisters every day, Valerie thought.

Saturday they both left work early. Valerie's spirits were high as she donned her new outfit, black velvet trousers and a silky white poet's blouse romantically ruffled at the wrists. Sexy red leather sandals with high heels made the most of her pretty ankles and feet. Her hair, helped along by a curling brush, swirled beautifully around her shoulders. But it didn't go with the image she was trying to create. Somewhat regretfully she wound it into a knot at the top of her head and pulled down long tendrils at her temples to soften the effect.

In front of the knot she pinned a white silk gardenia. Perfect, she decided. After a final check in the mirror, she picked up a red suede jacket and went to join Stephanie and her lanky young man.

They arrived at C.C.'s house on a wave of good spirits. As expected, Valerie thought the beautiful home a fine reflection of its owner. She fancied that she saw traits of his character in the strength of the foyer's glossy stone floors, in the clean-lined furniture covered in soft leathers and fine fabrics, in the gleam of brass and polished wood. A tall fireplace with a white marble hearth dominated the main living area; a custom-made rug with an Empire design defined it. Other conversational groupings were scattered about the long, multiwindowed room, and a window seat in an alcove invited solitary dreaming.

There were petite flower arrangements on tables, large ones on the mantel and on white octagonal pedestals. A huge vase of yellow roses and baby's breath graced the long dining room table just glimpsed in passing. She smiled, remembering how he'd once thought that fresh flowers all over the house meant impossible wealth.

Someone else had answered the door. She did not look for C.C. when she stepped into his house, yet he was the first person she saw, and for a suspended moment, the only one.

He looked shaken when their eyes met, then he was confidently in control again.

Stephanie had turned aside to greet someone. Valerie acknowledged the introductions her sister flung out, but her attention was riveted on C.C. He was all in black tonight, a handsome pirate come to claim his booty, she thought whimsically.

"Hello, Valerie," he said in the extraordinary deep voice that always made her skin tingle. "Welcome to my house."

"Thank you," she replied. "I'm delighted to be here, C.C."

She spoke reservedly, but C.C. didn't miss the huskiness pleasure gave to her voice. No matter how cool and collected she acted, he knew she was glad to see him. He hadn't missed the sparkle his presence had put in her eyes, either.

As for himself, he found it amazing the way she could brighten a room simply by walking into it.

He liked her sexy red shoes. But there was something besides sex in the allure of that simple black-and-white getup, something no other woman in the room possessed. That touch of class, he thought, then mentally shook his head. It was more than just class. It was also maturity. There were several, much younger women in the room. But they were merely green peaches on a limb where she hung sweet and ripe.

Someone claimed his attention just then, and Stephanie came hurrying back to finish the introductions to his other guests. She looked like a flame flitting among the soberly clad males who surrounded her. No wonder we provide such titillating speculation when we're together, he thought. Any man would go chasing after her given half a chance.

But his thoughts were fond, not lusty. Valerie was the one who had him tied up in lustful knots.

Fully aware of his swift but intense appraisal, though not of its content, Valerie refocused her attention as her sister asked proprietarily, "Want a tour of the house?"

"I'd love to see the house. But is it all right? Are you sure he won't mind us poking around his private quarters?"

"Of course I'm sure he won't mind. Others, maybe, but not you and me," Stephanie said with airy insouciance.

Valerie laughed in pleased agreement. She trailed after Stephanie through the large home, from a handsome study whose dark red walls were hung with artwork, to a library with three walls of books, a fireplace and a handsome leather chair complete with a cashmere afghan.

Silently Valerie followed her sister down a long hall to his private suite. The door was closed. They left it that way and retraced their steps, around the graceful curving staircase that led to the second floor, on down another short hall and into the shining white kitchen with its bright red accents.

Two Doric columns separated the living room from the television nook furnished with comfortable sofas and a handsome black leather lounger. Valerie thought it a wonderfully livable house. She wondered if anyone had shared it with him.

"Are you enjoying yourself?" C.C. asked, materializing at her side.

Startled, she stammered, "Y-yes, I am, very much. You have nice friends, C.C. And a lovely home."

"Some are just business acquaintances. But I agree, my friends are nice. I've known many of them for twenty years or more." His voice lowered. "And I'm glad you like my home. I worked real hard getting it to look like this."

"You, or a decorator?"

"Me. Oh, I had a decorator help out in some areas, but basically I did it myself. Finally brought all the stuff I've been collecting all these years into a semblance of order. But I don't pamper it, just relax and enjoy it," he went on expansively.

His voice lowered again, to intimacy. "Val, stay with me after everyone leaves." He grinned boyishly. "After all, I'll need a hand clearing up this mess, Yolanda will be going home as soon as she's cleaned the kitchen. Stay with me for a while."

Valerie bit her lip, tempted to consent, but not sure just what she'd be consenting to if she did. There was suddenly within her a joyous impatience to be alone with him, to relive again that immeasurable time of long, wet, sweet, warm kisses. Danger, she warned herself. But, oh, she wanted it!

Before she could frame an answer, he straightened with a host's smile as another couple joined them.

Several more people drifted into their circle. Valerie shifted from one foot to the other as she chatted with C.C. and his friends. The conversation was enjoyable, his guests entertaining, the wine superb. But C.C.'s nearness acted like a stimulant on her nerves and it was all she could do to keep from outright fidgeting.

The maid left. Around eleven o'clock other people began leaving, and in a few minutes they were down to Stephanie and her friend Bobby.

"Val, Bobby and I are going to stop by Alphonse's for a nightcap. Is that okay with you?" Stephanie asked.

C.C. answered. "Valerie hasn't got time to go gallivanting off to Alphonse's, she's helping me clean up this mess." He cocked an eyebrow at Stephanie. "Unless you're interested in helping, too? If not, I'll bring her home later."

"Not in the least interested. See you later, Val," Stephanie said breezily, and towed Bobby out the door.

"Later," Valerie echoed. She felt a conflicting sense of relief and annoyance that her mind had been made up for her.

She stood in the open doorway for a moment enjoying the cold air on her flushed face. She could feel C.C. behind her, feel his warmth, his powerful presence. The touch of his hand on her shoulder sent a tiny but potent shock through her entire system.

Slowly she closed the door.

C.C. reached around her and locked it.

She turned, and a second later found herself in his arms, being kissed with a lover's passion.

Eight

Valerie's head literally spun from the impact of C.C.'s hungry mouth. Her first instinct was to jerk away, but a deeper, more basic need took command as his powerful arms enwrapped her and pulled her so close she felt every muscle and fiber of his hard body. Warmth flooded her, a sweet, pulsing warmth, flowing alongside a spate of longing that shook her entire being.

She didn't resist him, couldn't resist him. The taste of him set off a blossoming explosion of excitement. With sensuous pleasure, she plunged her hands deep into his thick hair.

Gentleness threaded through his hunger. She felt it in his strong fingers, his breathtaking kisses. Through her velvet slacks she could feel the rougher cloth of his trousers, and beneath them, the sinewy planes of his solid male body. The contact filled her with a delicious ache.

At some point an icy sliver of sanity sliced through her pleasure. She had to stop, to somehow flatten this intoxicating excitement bubbling through her veins. But the hands on her back began moving down to more intimate flesh, an erotic stimulation that unleashed another passionate spring flood of longing. She stopped thinking and just felt, and it was wonderful.

For long, shimmering moments there was only the fiery delight of his demanding, taking, giving mouth, the pressure of the hard body straining into hers, his warm caresses. She loved the feel of his hair under her sensitive fingers. Her breathing became ragged. Merciless desire tightened her throat as he moved her against him. The incendiary pleasure of his expert hands made her shudder voluptuously.

But eventually those hands slid over her shoulders and down the front of her blouse. His touch on her breast acted as a shock of cold water.

Before she could gather her wits, he was already unfastening buttons, impatiently, fingers clumsy with the need to find the rounded flesh thrusting against thin fabric. The sound she made was a mixture of pain and pleasure.

Twisting aside, Valerie tore her mouth from his. "C.C., stop!" she gasped.

"No, honey," C.C. protested as she tried to pull away.

Shaken, she placed her palms flat on his chest. "Yes, I . . . please, C.C., don't," she said thinly, and lowered her face to his shoulder. She felt him trembling and that was lovely. She drew in air and let a relieving shiver flow down her body. Confusedly she realized she didn't want to leave the haven of his arms regardless of what she said. "Just hold me," she half pleaded. "That's all I need, just to be held."

C.C. buried his face in her fragrant hair and breathed a shuddery sigh. "And I need to hold you," he said thickly. "But I need to hold you in my bed, all warm and naked and ready for love. I can't just go on wanting you and doing nothing about it, Val."

A fiery anger flared in Valerie's heart. She didn't know what it stemmed from or where it was aimed. But she did hate being made to feel guilty. "Don't pressure me, C.C.," she said, dead level. "I'm too old and too sensible to be affected by male pressuring."

"Valerie, I wasn't pressuring you—"

Her chin snapped up; hot dark eyes glared into his. "Yes, you were. You've been doing that ever since we met, subtly, but pressure, nonetheless."

C.C. dropped his arms and stepped back, a flinty touch of arrogance shading his voice. "I don't *pressure* women. I don't need to." His head tilted. "You think maybe you could be mistaking a simple expression of desire for what you call pressure?" he asked shrewdly, eyes glinting as her mouth twisted in denial to his words.

But Valerie felt confused again and her defiance rapidly melted away, leaving only stubborn, inarticulate anger. "I think I know the difference," she said coldly. She walked around him, into the living room. "Look, I stayed to help clean up."

"Did you?" he slipped in softly.

She flushed. "Well, I didn't stay for sex," she said with wintry dryness. "Let's get started on this shall we? I'd like to go home."

"Oh, leave it. Yolanda can get it in the morning," he replied with noticeable irritation.

Angrily penitent, she protested, "But I don't mind, C.C. It won't take but a few minutes."

"No. Let me get your coat and I'll take you home."

Silenced by his flat tone, she shrugged and waited while he got her red jacket.

The ride home was fraught with awkward silences. C.C. hated it. We're two mature adults, he thought, annoyed at how uncomfortable he felt. We should be able to handle this, damn it! It's no big deal. But it *was* a big deal—her accusation had hurt him far more than it had any right to. In fact, the depth of his emotions kept stunning him, especially his passionate need for her. He had expected fireworks, but not that magnificence of feeling, not that trembling pain. He had wanted her with all of him, not just his needful body.

And still wanted. He sighed to himself as he breathed in the flowery scent that clung to his shirt. But at least he was back in control again. Confused—for he thought he'd been open and honest with her about his feelings—but in control enough to apologize and try to understand her side of it at least.

"Valerie, I'm sorry that you felt I was rushing you," he said stiffly. "But you can't pretend you didn't want me as much as I wanted you. I've had too much experience to make a mistake like that."

"I'm not pretending anything," Valerie replied wearily. "I wanted you, all right. I still do. But I..." She sighed. At the moment she was simply not capable of explanations. "I can't."

His voice softened. "Why not, Val? Logically there's nothing to stop us."

"I know. But sometimes I don't respond to logic. Women often don't, you know," she said, trying to inject some humor into the situation.

It didn't work. "Grown women do," he countered flatly. His breath made a small explosion of sound in the quiet car. "I'm not accustomed to this sort of thing, so would you please tell me. Just what's with you, anyway? You give every evidence of liking me, of welcoming my advances, then you throw up a wall every time I try to get close. You say you see my logic, yet you refuse to explain what's stopping you from making love with me. You won't even talk to me about it. What is all this secretiveness about, Val? Why are you so scared of getting close?"

"I'm not *scared* of anything," she shot back, feeling argumentative again. So he wasn't accustomed to rejection—was he such a great lover, then? Jealousy speared her—did years of tomcat practice make perfect? Her voice took on a caustic edge. "What's so astonishing about me not wanting to make love with you, C.C.? Surely you've been rebuffed before, at least once!"

"You think that's what all this is about—me being rebuffed and resenting it?"

The fight went out of her. "No, I don't think that's what this is about," she said on a weary sigh. Thank God they were pulling into her driveway! As soon as he stopped the car, she opened the door and started to get out, then paused for a bit of solid truth. "And I do like you, C.C., you know that. I'm just...just not ready for anything more than this."

He stared at her for an agonizingly long moment. Then he shrugged. "Well, I guess if you're not, you're not."

His words were still preying on her mind and heart as Valerie undressed and rehung her clothes. With dragging movements she took off her underwear, then sat down on the bed and massaged her throbbing temples. She still felt the muddy swirl of anger and frustration. But it was directed at herself, not C.C. Why hadn't she simply sat down with him and discussed her feelings? *And why hadn't she told him the source of those feelings!*

Trying to get a grip on her emotions, she reminded herself that she was leaving day after tomorrow to spend Thanksgiving weekend with her children. She'd have ample time to think about it then, to make decisions. Besides, came the furtive thought, if she told him now, there might not be anything to come back to.

Maybe there wasn't, anyway. With unsettling urgency, she went over the scene again, trying to ascertain his true feelings. Despite their heated argument, he'd sounded almost indifferent after it was over. But was he? He was a man of strong passions. Could he really shrug off her anger and rejection so easily? Or would it create an awkward barrier between them? She didn't know, but she supposed she'd find out one way or another.

Unease mingled with her anger. She hated her inner turmoil. But she knew that most of the pressure she was feeling came from herself. The decision to relocate, to give up the old and familiar and safe for the uncertainty of a new life, was an enormous source of pressure in itself. Then, after she was comfortably certain that that part of her life was over and she was safe from the danger of more heartbreak, there was C.C. and the explosive emotions he aroused.

She shuddered as recall swamped her and those feelings came violently alive again. She closed her eyes and placed a hand against her mouth to stifle a soft cry. Her body ached. It burned in places, needful and wanting. A woman's need. But she had acted like a confused girl tonight, denying them their rightful passion because of fear.

She got up and went into the bathroom to brush her teeth. But her naked image caught and held her attention. So vulnerable, she thought. And suddenly she was bent over weeping, hard, desolate sobs that tore at her throat and wracked her body.

A terrible sense of anguish and loss gripped her heart. She wrapped her arms around herself, rocking back and forth, gasping with the pain that seemed to be dredged up from some deep, subterranean well. It overwhelmed her until she feared she'd drown in her river of tears.

Her appallingly undisciplined weeping was shaming to a woman who had rarely cried once she'd gotten through the first dreary weeks of adjustment. Then, slowly, that raw emotion melted into soft, sorrowed realization. She still wept, but that was nothing to be ashamed of. At long last she was mourning, mourning the death of a lovely, living breast.

"Valerie, you don't have to come to work this morning—sleep late if you want," Stephanie chided the next morning when her sister stumbled into the kitchen, yawning prodigiously. "I didn't mean for this to be a nine-to-five job, anyway. God knows your financial help was contribution enough. You bailed us out, love. It's purely selfish of me to ask for more."

She poured her sleepy-eyed sister a cup of coffee. "Anyway, when the kids get here, you'll want to stay home with them. Or at least modify your working hours to fit theirs."

Practically inhaling her coffee, Valerie held out the cup for a refill. Stephanie, having just come in from her morning run, was still dressed in T-shirt, jogging shorts and shoes. She looked incredibly sexy in the abbreviated outfit, Valerie thought.

"I agree, honey," she said, "but the kids aren't here and I am. I told you I want to be *useful,* Steffie, not just a dilettante."

"You're useful," Stephanie protested. "Val, you've been a lifesaver to me, in more ways than you realize, I think. I don't know how I'd have gotten through this mess with Randy without you."

Valerie shook her head. "I don't know that I helped all that much."

"Oh, yes, you did. And you're a big help at the nursery, too."

Valerie doubted it. She had slept poorly and was not in the mood to be easy on herself. Besides, for all her efforts, she hadn't really found her place in the business yet. Half the time she couldn't even answer customer questions. She didn't know what was where, had no idea how to recommend landscaping shrubs or trees to suit a particular site and was probably nowhere near worth the salary Stephanie insisted she draw. Any of the salesgirls—who worked cheaper—could do it better, she thought dejectedly.

Her mood was so low that she had to make a conscious effort to bring herself up. Tomorrow she'd be leaving for Louisiana and her holiday weekend, and she was looking forward to that. It would be so good to see the kids again, to hold them in her arms and hug them to her heart's content!

"Val, I heard you crying last night," Stephanie said hesitantly. "I wanted to come to you, but something told me that I'd be intruding, that this was private weeping."

"Yes, it was, honey. Very private weeping, the kind that should have been done years ago," Valerie said with a wry little smile.

Having no appetite, she put down her cinnamon roll and went back to her room to shower. As she dried off, she brought the towel slowly down her chest and over the breast C.C. had touched last night. Her skin tingled there as she remembered the feel of his hand cradling the soft curve. But the area of the mastectomy was numb since the nerves that supplied sensation there had been removed with her breast. The inside of her upper arm was also numb and she dried it reflectively.

Letting C.C. kiss me like that last night was pure foolishness, she thought, bringing down the towel. I can't let anyone get this close to me. How could they stand looking at me? *I* can't even stand looking at me. I look down, I look to the side. I can't stand in front of a mirror and look at myself.

Time should make a difference. But time hasn't. I still hurt when I see what they've done to me.

Steeling herself, she traced the scar with one finger. Then she turned from the mirror and began dressing.

* * *

Her spirits lifted as she made herself useful around the nursery. After lunch she went out to the large greenhouse behind the shop, her favorite place to work. The greenhouse supervisor soon put her to the task of unboxing and positioning a shipment of exotic plants, and time passed quickly.

As she worked, Valerie's thoughts ran on, with little puffs of excitement marking some new proposal. There was room for improvement here, too. The greenhouse was a simple building, covered with weather-stained and mildewed fiberglass that should have been replaced long ago. A wood-chip-floored aisle sliced through the center of the long structure, with rough wood benches on each side holding myriad plants.

A hodgepodge of other plants sat at the back of the building. There was no style, no real staging effects. It should look like a fairyland in here, she thought. Instead, it's faintly like being underwater.

"It's not in the least inviting," she said to Stephanie during their coffee break.

"I know it, but... money, you know." Stephanie sighed.

"I can get more money," Valerie said. "Enough to make the most needed improvements, anyway. I'll start keeping a list of ideas that come to me," she ended on a jaunty note that made them both smile.

The day had become chill and overcast, and customers were few. Around four Stephanie suggested, "Since you'll be leaving tomorrow, let's celebrate tonight. You go on home and make us one of your scrumptious dinners! I'll pick up some wine."

"Okay. I'll make us a nice meatloaf," Valerie said in a way that caused Stephanie to burst out laughing. After a startled instant, Valerie began to laugh, too.

"Mother!" they exclaimed simultaneously.

Valerie gave another joyous little laugh as they shared a childhood memory. Their mother had used meatloaf as a panacea like other women used a cup of hot tea.

Stephanie sobered. "I missed her so much after she died. You were already out in the world, already had your own family. But me, I was still coming home from school every day, and she wasn't there anymore."

Valerie's eyes stung. "I'm sorry, honey. Looks like both of us failed each other in important ways. But it won't happen again, Stephanie," she assured her quietly.

"No, it won't, for either of us. Well!" Stephanie shook off her momentary sadness. "Listen, why don't you cook enough for, oh, three or four more people? We'll have us a little party!"

"You party animal, you," Valerie said, laughing. "But all right, I'll cook—you invite the people."

"Okay... anyone you want me to ask?"

Valerie hesitated. "No, ask whoever you choose," she said. She was a little nervous about seeing C.C. again.

On the way home she stopped at the supermarket for the ingredients of a simple meatloaf napped with a sauce of sweet red peppers. A passionate-colored sauce, she thought, mouth curving as she considered its lovely crimson hue. Was passion red? Not quite, she decided. More like the colors of flame, orange and gold and hot. She shivered, recalling the fiery delight of C.C.'s kisses last night. But when he'd touched her breast...

She refused to think about it; she had a meal to cook, and company coming.

After unloading her groceries, she took a quick shower and redressed in a bulky ski sweater and pleated slacks. Her hair was brushed out and left loose around her face. On a whim she threaded a pink ribbon through the russet mass and tied a bow just above one ear. Silly but festive, she decided. Leaving it there, she returned to the kitchen.

Along with the spicy meatloaf and its velvety sauce, she made oven-roasted potatoes and concocted a splendid salad from fresh spinach, sweet red onion and mandarin orange slices, to be served with a warm vinegar-and-bacon dressing. She had forgotten to pick up garlic bread and had to dash back to the market.

It was drizzling and traffic was heavy. By the time she returned home, Stephanie was there. So was C.C. Valerie stopped with a jolt of excitement mixed with anxiety. But he was laughing, mustache quirking, blue eyes twinkling up and down her lissome form.

Relief shot through her. Obviously he had shrugged off last night's scene. Well, of course, she scolded her anxious self. He's a man, not some twenty-year-old who's pouting because he didn't get his way.

A moment later, as their gazes tangled, she was uncertain again. Something dark and shadowed flickered at the back of his eyes.

Before greeting him, she pulled off her jacket and hung it on the coat tree. Her hair had gotten tangled by the wind. Smoothing it, she smiled and said, "Hello, C.C. I didn't expect to see you here tonight."

"Steph'nie took pity," he said. "I was just going to open a can of soup tonight. Thank goodness she changed my mind. Whatever you're cooking smells wonderful!"

Valerie flushed with pleasure. Casting him a wry glance, she told Stephanie, "I think men just like me for my cooking. Who else is coming?"

"Just Bobby. One each—I thought that would be nice," Stephanie said impishly.

Feeling ambivalent about her sister's remark, Valerie commanded, "Come help me in the kitchen. C.C., make yourself at home. Do you need anything, do you have a drink?"

C.C. sat back down and gave her a lazy smile. "I have a drink," he said, lifting the beer Stephanie had given him. "I can make do with this, for now."

Giving him a sharp glance, Valerie nodded and went on to the kitchen. "Stephanie, would you please carry the conversation tonight?" she asked tersely. "C.C. and I had a little disagreement last night and I still feel awkward about it, though he evidently does not."

"What did you disagree about?"

"Never mind," Valerie answered tartly. "If you would please just take care of any prickly silences, I'd appreciate it."

Containing her rampant curiosity, Stephanie let her off with a breezy, "Will do."

Bobby, a mild-mannered man in his late twenties with long, pale brown hair, arrived a few minutes later and they sat down to dinner. True to her word, Stephanie kept the conversation light and lively, freeing her sister of the restraint she felt. After the fine meal, they all cleared the table, then adjourned to the living room with wine and a cheese tray.

"Steph'nie says you're going home tomorrow," C.C. said to Valerie. "Funny you didn't mention it last night."

"Not home, exactly," Valerie replied, overlooking the rest of his statement. C.C.'s blue shirt made his eyes look even more vivid. She avoided catching his gaze. "I'm spending the holiday at the children's school, with Nana," she continued smoothly. "Most of the other children will go home, but there'll be a few who won't, so she must stay, too. I didn't want to leave her alone, so..." She lifted her shoulders.

"While you're gone, I'm going apartment hunting," Stephanie stepped in.

Valerie looked surprised. "What on earth for? This house is certainly big enough for both of us."

"Logistically it is. But I think we both need our space. So I'm going to start keeping an eye out for something special. Besides, it'll be neat having an apartment. Do you realize I've lived in this house all my life?"

Valerie smiled at her indignant tone. This had been Stephanie's father's house. "That long, hmm?" she teased.

Everyone laughed. A few minutes later, Stephanie and Bobby decided to go out for a while.

Valerie drew her aside. "Stephanie, you've been out late nearly every night this week," she protested.

"And I'm going to be out late again tonight," Stephanie said airily. But her eyes were too bright. "I try to postpone going to bed as long as possible, because you think too much in bed. Okay, big sister?"

"Okay, honey. I didn't mean to be so heavy-handed, I was just concerned about you."

"Thanks, but there's no need to be. I'm okay," Stephanie asserted. "Hey, you and C.C. can come with us if you want."

"I don't know about C.C.," Valerie said, glancing at him, "but one late night is enough for me. I think I'll turn in early."

Her gaze met his as she spoke, and a sensuous electricity arced between them. His jaw squared, C.C. gave laconic agreement.

The younger couple left shortly afterward. Taking his time, C.C. got his coat and shrugged it on. Valerie kept a small distance from him. The tight smile she maintained flooded him with annoyance.

"Don't look so worried, Valerie. You're quite safe, no more grabbing and kissing you, I promise," he drawled. But she looked so young and vulnerable with that pink ribbon in her hair. His mockery dried in his mouth. "At least I promise to try," he said with a low, teasing laugh. Her

mouth softened; ample reward for his efforts, he thought.
"Have a good holiday, Val."

"You, too."

"Yes, I think I will," he murmured, looking thoughtful.
He lifted her hand and touched it to his lips. "I'll see you
when you get back."

"Yes, when I get back," she said.

The twins had grown astonishingly, Valerie thought, and
she cried a little when they came racing out the door to meet
her on the school's front lawn. They were delighted to see
one another, and there was much hugging and kissing before Valerie had had her fill of holding them. Then the
chatter began, until the living room of Nana's tiny apartment rang with it.

They'd gotten their hair cut and looked so much older.
"But it looks beautiful—you look beautiful— God, I've
missed you two!" she exclaimed, sweeping them into her
arms again. They seemed to be all legs and arms, rangy, like
their parents, but still soft and cuddly enough to hold forever. She allowed a fleeting wonder about C.C.'s reaction to
them. *Would* he be a good father? Quickly she banished the
thought.

A little hesitantly, watching their bright little faces as she
spoke, Valerie told them of her decision to move to Texas.
To her vast relief, both girls seemed very excited about the
prospect of a new life. They talked it through while afternoon shadows lengthened on the parklike schoolgrounds.

"I had all *A*s on my report card," Bonnie said in re-
minder of the deal they'd made: a dollar for each *A*.

Valerie paid up.

"Well, I took a first in gymnastics," Brenda reminded
her. "See, here's my ribbon!"

Brenda and *A*s seemed totally incompatible. "A first-
place ribbon is certainly worth a dollar," Valerie declared.

She smiled at the tall woman with beautiful white hair who came in bearing a tray of tea and homemade scones. Nana, though a citizen by marriage, was English by birth. She still loved her four-o'clock tea.

Valerie, who wasn't a tea drinker by choice, indulged her, for she loved her mother-in-law. Besides, Nana had taught the children the proper way with tea, and it was pleasurable to watch them pouring the fragrant brew, then fixing it up with a lump of sugar and a dollop of milk, and daintily sipping the finished product.

"Then you've definitely decided to live in Texas?" the older woman, whose name was Elizabeth, asked in her inimitable English-Southern accent.

"Yes, I think it is definite," Valerie replied. "I'll be moving right after Christmas."

"Hooray!" the twins yelled.

They were so eager to take on anything new, Valerie thought as she watched them. And so trusting that their mother knew what she was doing. When they went back to their own pursuits, Valerie said, "I think Brenda is much more the young lady, Nana. You're doing a good job with that little rapscallion."

Graciously Elizabeth Hepburn accepted the compliment and poured more tea. "I'm sure Texas is grand and all that, but tell me, my dear, how do you really feel about starting a new life there?"

"Scared. Uncertain. But excited, too."

Dusk gathered under the high ceilings as the two women talked on. But Valerie didn't mention C.C. at all.

On Thanksgiving they prepared a small turkey with all the trimmings. Nana was a football fan, and after dinner Valerie companionably watched the games with her. But her thoughts weren't in this cozy little room. Mentally she was miles away, in a big house in Texas. What was C.C. doing for Thanksgiving? Eating alone? Or going out to dinner? By himself? Or with a woman? The redhead, perhaps. Jealousy again. She decided to stop thinking about C.C.

But that night in bed she discovered she didn't have a choice in the matter. C.C. was there in her mind's eye, smiling that quizzical little smile she sometimes saw on his fine mouth when she caught him watching her. His body had felt good against hers, vibrant with sensual promise. She thought of his hands, so strong and hard and knowing, yet so gentle, so aware of her fragility. Desire trickled through her, catching hurtfully in her stomach, leaving her to fall asleep filled with longing.

The next day was her birthday, and they had a wild celebration, complete with champagne—a tiny glassful for each of the girls, half a bottle for her.

Bonnie's present was a laboriously cross-stitched picture extolling Home Sweet Home.

Brenda's was a pair of rhinestone-studded lizard earrings.

Valerie declared both gifts beautiful.

Forty, she thought. I'm forty. In her slightly tipsy state of mind, it seemed an ancient age.

As the girls got ready for bed that night, Bonnie asked wistfully, "Mom, do you think me and Brenda could come to Texas at Christmas and see our new house?"

"Yes, darling. The week after Christmas we'll spend in Texas. But I want us to spend Christmas itself in our old home, among familiar surroundings and friends."

Brenda's interest took a different turn. "Mom, do you have a boyfriend down there in Texas?"

Valerie answered carefully, "Well, I have a friend and he's a boy as opposed to a girl, so you might say that. Would you mind if I did?"

"Heck, no, I think it's neat," her bright-eyed child declared.

"I said *if* I did, remember? Now hush and go to bed so I can get some sleep, too. We're going shopping tomorrow, and you know that always wears me out," she admonished the giggling little girls.

Still feeling slightly light-headed and more brave than usual, Valerie went to her own room to think, not sleep. That remark about a boyfriend was bothersome, to say the least. Forty years old and the mother of two children, she reflected. Not exactly a romantic thing to be. Any man would prefer one of those free-as-the-wind young lovelies to a practically middle-aged lady with kids...

But C.C. wasn't just any man, she reminded herself with a soft and wistful smile. He deserved to know why she was so skittish about a sexual relationship. It was time to tell him about her surgery.

But she was going through agony just imagining it. Standing in front of the mirror, she wondered how to tell him. Dramatically, with tears, perhaps even a few hysterics? Or cool and casual, maybe even a little witty. *"Oh, by the way, I've had a mastectomy so I'm a little one-sided...."*

She shuddered. How would he react when she did tell him? In a manly fashion, or at least what he'd consider a manly fashion? Commiserating with her while trying to conceal his fastidious distaste at the picture she would be drawing for him?

Another man had acted like that. Maybe C.C. wouldn't want her anymore, either.

Her eyelids stung. I'm vulnerable, so vulnerable, she thought with a quivery sigh. Hastily she pulled on her flannel nightshirt. Maybe he would be too embarrassed to even discuss such an indelicate subject as a woman's breasts...

"Oh, damn!" she muttered. It was nerve-racking to realize that she had no idea how he would take it.

But one thing was certain: she *was* going to tell him.

Nine

C.C. couldn't believe it. Whether he was on the job watching the minutes fall like drops of lead into a bottomless bucket, or sitting in his study listening to the water-torture slowness of a ticking clock, he couldn't believe how much he was missing Valerie Hepburn.

It wasn't just her lovely body, though God knew he missed that. Just thinking of her perfect face and form created a pulsing warmth in deep, secret places. Remembering how soft she felt and how delicious she tasted could, and did, ignite little fires throughout his long frame.

But he missed her sweet presence, too, like sunshine to his soul. He missed her soft smile and quick humor, the little laugh that erupted through her lips as if surprised out of its hiding place by his cleverness. He missed her low, honeyed voice. He just missed *her*.

But what really bothered him was how much he wanted to see her. That's all, just see her. And talk. And laugh. And

then catch her in his arms and kiss her until this fierce ache
went away.

She had left on Wednesday. It was now Sunday afternoon. He could call her, but what if she wasn't home yet?
What would he say to Stephanie? He felt like a teenager
again, scared to call his girlfriend's house in case he got her
father on the phone.

Ridiculous. He'd spoken to Stephanie dozens of times on
the telephone. But he'd never asked for Valerie before.

"Damn!" he swore, glancing at the clock again. He
couldn't believe himself, either, acting like a moony, love-
sick youth.

He shied away from the word love. He supposed nothing
else frightened a man as much as that little word. But Valerie's prolonged absence had changed him. It had him
wondering, with absurd anxiety, if she really was coming
back.

It had also changed his way of looking at certain things,
such as falling in love and marrying again. Not that he intended doing either one. But the possibility didn't seem so
remote now. And willing or not, he had to admit that he already liked her far more than he'd thought possible to ever
care for another woman.

The admission shook him. He didn't want to go down
that white-water river again. But he had an unsettling suspicion that he was already on it.

With sudden resolve he reached for the telephone, then
put down the receiver and stood. He was embarrassing
himself. He was too old to be acting like this over a woman.
He had the requisite little black bachelor's book with its list
of amenable females. Any one of them would make a suitable companion for the long, lonely evening stretching out
ahead of him.

But he didn't follow through on his frustrated impulse.
There was only *one* woman he wanted to be with. He wished

it was different, for he didn't really like feeling this way. It was aggravating to admit that he hadn't the foggiest idea how to stop this wild slide into trouble.

He sat down again. Time crept by. As distractions, the luxury of fine brandy in a Baccarat snifter and a mellow Havana cigar were useful. Better than nothing, anyway. He turned on the television. Tomorrow he'd call. Soon enough, he told himself.

But tomorrow was an eternity in coming.

At noon the next day he called the nursery and asked for Valerie. Then, when she came on the line, the only thing he could think of to say was "You're back."

"Yes, I got in late yesterday evening."

She wouldn't have been home if I had called her yesterday, he congratulated his excellent judgment.

"Did you have a good holiday?" he asked.

"Yes, very good," she said.

And then she said, "But I missed you."

"You missed me?"

Her low, rich chuckle tickled intimately.

"Yes, I missed you. In fact, I missed this place. I was glad to get back." Her hesitation was barely perceptible. "C.C., if you're not busy tonight, I'd like to see you. I've something I want to tell you."

She sounded so serious, his imagination raced. "What, that you've taken up again with an old boyfriend?" he half jested.

"No. I don't have an old boyfriend," she said simply. "I just want to see you. But if you're busy..."

"If I was, I'm not now. I'll pick you up at...seven? What are you in the mood for?" he added so archly that he slapped his forehead. *Idiot!*

"Just some brandy and talk at your house."

"Sounds good to me. What kind of brandy? Apple, peach, raspberry?"

"Raspberry sounds lovely. See you at seven?"

"Seven sharp."

She laughed. "Seven sharp."

C.C. hung up slowly, reflectively. What did she want to tell him? Nothing serious, he assured himself. She'd probably only known one man in her life and the reason for her sexual hangups was her lack of experience. Very likely she'd never felt anything like the tremendous attraction between them and was having trouble handling it. Since he didn't believe in borrowing trouble, he refused to indulge in darker speculations.

He set the matter aside in favor of another. Only seven hours to go and he'd be seeing her. He tilted back his office chair, his expression bemused. He didn't understand this crazy rush of exhilaration fizzing in his bloodstream. Except that she was one of a kind, and he was a man who appreciated the unique.

The thought relieved him. He picked up his hat and got on with business.

Clad in a slip, Valerie twisted around to frown at her sister's sly smile. "Stephanie, for heaven's sake, we're only going to talk a bit and enjoy some brandy at his house."

"Of course you are."

"We *are*. Now stop grinning like a Cheshire cat and get out of here and let me get dressed. It's almost seven and you know how prompt C.C. is."

"Do I ever!" Stephanie picked up the white fur mound that was Dempsey, who was lying on the bed watching it all with a cat's curious delight. "Val? Have I told you how glad I am to have you back here?"

"Yes, about as many times as I've said how glad I am to be back. Now shoo," Valerie said exasperatedly. She felt too unguarded and edgy to answer her sister's questions, or to endure her good-hearted teasing. It was a point of honor not to betray how nervous she was just thinking about tonight, much less talking about it.

Even though hurried, she still took time to brush her hair until it shone with highlights. Leaving it to drift around her shoulders, she slithered into a simple green silk jersey frock that skimmed the body and nipped in at the waist with a narrow, self-fabric sash. A long center slit allowed glimpses of silken leg. The back draped low enough to reveal an expanse of creamy skin while the cowl front covered her entire throat. She felt sexy tonight and wanted to look it. She also felt so jittery she jumped a foot when Dempsey poured himself between her ankles.

Outwardly she was cool and composed when she walked into the den to greet C.C. But her inner self trembled with the little shock of delight at just seeing this magnificent man again, so tall and trim, his eyes so startlingly blue against the sun-gilded richness of hair and skin. He was dressed casually, in an open-throat white shirt, blue sports jacket and navy slacks worn with supple leather boots. Yet there was an air of authority about him that could dominate any room.

He and Stephanie were standing by the television set, laughing about something. Valerie's helpless rush of gladness was tinged with anxiety as she strolled toward them. When he saw her, the curve of his mouth subtly altered, making the smile he gave her seem blindingly sweet and intimate. But since Stephanie apparently saw nothing amiss, she put it down to imagination.

Just the same she gave those alert green eyes a look that sent Stephanie out of the room on a just-remembered errand.

"Hello, Valerie," C.C. said. His smile deepened as his gaze ran over her. "Welcome back. It's good to see you again."

"And you," Valerie replied with a catch of breath.

She had just discovered that a woman's heart could beat as fast at forty as it could at twenty.

She passed him her coat and he helped her on with it. His hands lingered on her shoulders, and for just an instant she leaned back into their beguiling strength.

Carefully he lifted her hair from under the shawl collar. "I like your hair like this, all soft and loose. But I also like it up, all prim and ladylike." His eyes crinkled. "Maybe because the two offer such intriguing contrasts."

"Thank you for sharing that thought with me, C.C.," she said dryly. Smiling with pleasure at the sound of his deep laugh, she walked with him under the sweep of black, starry skies to his car.

He was driving his big Lincoln, but it was amazing how space shrunk when he was next to her. She could smell his clean scent, feel his vibrant warmth. When he turned to speak to her, the dim dash light and open-collared shirt worked together to afford her a glimpse of the tight gold curls at the base of his strong throat. Imagine kissing there, she thought, and hurriedly focused her gaze back to the window.

"I've been going slightly crazy today wondering what you have to tell me," C.C. remarked.

Chagrined, she said, "C.C., I didn't mean to drive you crazy. It's not...that is..." She shook her head. "We'll discuss it at the house. In the den, while we're relaxing with our brandy."

"That bad, huh?"

"No, not that bad," she protested, feeling her cheeks grow hotter. "It's just that, well, you asked me what caused my so-called secretiveness and I thought I'd tell you, that's all."

"No big deal, then," he said with a swift, searching glance.

Valerie wished she could say that. But it was looming larger and larger with every mile that passed. She wished she had never brought it up at all. "You'll have to judge for yourself," she replied with forced ease.

On impulse she laid her hand on his thigh. Too bold? His fingers covered hers and squeezed. Deliberately relaxing, she began telling him about her visit with the children. He listened with pleasing interest, especially to their reaction to the move.

"It's definite, then?" he double-checked.

"It's definite. What did you do over the holiday?" she asked as they turned down his street.

"Visited California."

"You went to see Jordan? How did it go?"

"As well as could be expected, I guess. Actually, maybe a little better. He already had plans, but he did invite me to have Thanksgiving dinner with him."

"And his mother?"

"No, she still lives in Europe. Just him and me. It wasn't any great breakthrough, but at least we did talk."

"That's a start, C.C. It'll work out, you'll see," she responded in her softest voice.

"I guess time will tell," C.C. said, dismissing the touchy subject. Only too aware of her touch, he drove into his garage and cut the motor. "Well, here we are," he said huskily. "Are you game to step into this spider's parlor, little fly?"

Casually she withdrew her hand and picked up her purse. "I've never been particularly afraid of spiders."

Marking the seductive quality of her low laugh, he felt a rich throb of excitement. After we talk, he decided with a heated rush of blood, after we talk we'll make love.

They settled in the luxurious den, near the small round table C.C. had set up. It held a gorgeous brandy decanter, crystal snifters, a silver bowl of nuts and another holding Chinese fortune cookies.

"A weakness of mine," he confessed. "I buy them by the box!"

He passed the bowl and she took one, thinking she would enjoy his little idiosyncrasy far more if she didn't have this knot in her throat. The brandy was like a delicious, raspberry fire burning a lovely streak all the way to her toes. She needed its warmth; she felt cold inside.

To her amusement, C.C. was boyishly impatient to open his fortune cookie.

"Now?" he asked, watching her unwrap hers.

"Now."

"Ah," he said as he read the tiny slip of paper folded inside the waxy little cookie. "It says, 'You are master of all you survey tonight.'" Leaning toward her, he leered, stroking his mustache fiendishly. "I'm surveying you masterfully right this minute." When she didn't look too impressed, he asked, "What does yours say?"

"I will live long and prosper, according to this."

"A very good fortune."

A half smile touched her lips. "Yes, it is." Rising, she walked to the table for another shot of brandy. She loved the luscious stuff. "May I pour you some more?" she inquired.

"Please." C.C. joined her at the table. He took both glasses and set them down on the white linen cloth. Before she could question, he drew her into his arms and kissed her for a long, lovely time.

She felt so good in his arms, and he was so hungry for the taste and feel of her. With great effort, he restrained his raging urges. She was responding, but there was a tension in her fine body that he hadn't felt before. Gently he held her, suddenly remembering the first time he had embraced this startling delicacy of bone and flesh. He still felt the same secret sense of awe.

When he released her lips and she looked up at him, even her face seemed to have tautened. His skin prickled. Was something wrong, he wondered, followed instantly by the thought, If it is, I'll fix it.

With a slight push against his chest, she freed herself and moved away from him, to one of the chairs flanking the hearth. He took the other.

"So what's your deep, dark secret, Ms. Hepburn?" he asked teasingly. "Do you belong to a nudist colony? Or grow a fur coat when the moon is full? Don't tell me, you have a wooden leg," he said with mock horror.

To his astonishment, her face drained of color. Rendered speechless, he stared at her, registering with some part of him other than his brain the pain in her lovely eyes. Even as it happened he was coming to his feet, reaching out to her.

She held up a hand to stay his intent. "No, not a wooden leg," she said with a smile so wry he felt it in his chest. She clasped her hands together. "God, I don't know how to do this, where to begin."

He sank back down, suddenly no longer sure he could fix it, conscious of a quill of fear where only seconds ago had dwelt a surety of purpose.

"Just say it, honey," he said softly, encouragingly.

"Very well." Drawing an audible breath, she spoke swiftly, without inflection. "A year or so ago, a routine mammogram showed a lump in my breast. The biopsy proved malignant: I had cancer. So I had a mastectomy. The entire breast was removed. There was a bright side to it: the cancer was caught early and there was no sign of metastasis, which meant that I could expect five-year disease-free survival."

C.C. had become so still that his muscles felt like glass, easily shattered with a sharp movement. "My God, Val," he said like a breath of prayer. Her words had wiped his mind clean, and those dark eyes were so huge and watchful. She needed something from him, reassuring words, but even if he could come up with some, there was the appalling chance that she might misinterpret them.

Shifting his tense frame, he swore softly. He couldn't dwell on what she'd just told him—*she* needed his attention right now. But his brain clung tenaciously to the terrible threat to her life. He let out his breath with an audible rush. She's all right, he told himself firmly. He knew that a recurrence was always possible, but she had to be all right. It was unthinkable that she might not be. Gazing into those beautiful brown eyes, opened unflinchingly wide and direct, he felt an almost overwhelming compulsion to carry her to his bedroom and ravish her with love.

But passion was shoved aside as a new, more violent fire seared his heart. She needed comforting, not lovemaking. She needed to be held and protected. And he needed to do it.

Slowly he rose and took her hands; carefully he drew her into his arms. Her body was stiff in his embrace. "I'm so sorry it happened, honey," he said, unbearably husky. "But so glad you're all right, and going to be all right. And you are, Valerie, you are."

Her lips curved, acknowledging his fervent insistence. He tightened his grip, both on her shoulders and on himself. He would not give into emotion. "Since we've definitely, absolutely settled that, what's the problem?" he asked, forcibly light.

"The problem is that surgery left me with a terrible disfigurement. For several reasons I was in a pretty wretched state of mind at the time and so I ... didn't bother with reconstructive surgery. So while I don't have a wooden leg, I do have a prosthesis."

"Val, I'm sorry about that dumb remark!" He groaned. "It was just my stupid way of trying to put you at ease. Anyway, I repeat, what's the problem?"

"The problem is that I lost a breast, C.C.," she replied with strained patience.

"Oh, Val, that doesn't matter—"

"Stop it! I hate it when people tell me that. It *does* matter—it matters to me! And it matters to others, too." Her head lowered. "At least it did to one man. We were attracted to each other, but it went nowhere ... because my surgery turned him off. I don't hold that against him, one can't help how one feels about something." She looked up at him. "It might change your mind about me, too."

"Val ..." Pain gouged his throat and he had to clear it. Her dark gaze was still fixed on his face, her eyes alert, chin turned slightly as if to deflect a verbal blow. Questions churned in his mind. He blocked them. "Val, it won't change my mind, won't change the way I feel about you," he said with gratifying firmness.

Her mouth twisted.

"Oh, here," he said. "Here, let me hold you, just hold you." He pulled her close and warm, trying with his fierce embrace to pour all the healing strength of his body into hers. He intended burying his wanting mouth in her hair. But her face was upturned, her lips so near, and he had to kiss her or die.

The taste of her was fuel to passion's fire. On the instant, desire welled up to flood him with raw, primal urges. Her lips parted, her tongue sought his and the body he now held in his arms was suddenly soft and pliant. It seemed to spread down his front, wrapping around his maleness until he had to stifle a groan. He was kissing her with wild hunger, and everything in him that was male wanted her with its own savage insistence.

But that wasn't what *she* needed. He stopped kissing her and rested his lips against her smooth brow while he drew the steadying breaths that would let him remember that. Comfort and protect, he reminded himself. Soothe, be sensitive, be compassionate. His mind was a little hazed, but he was sure that was the right thing to do for her at this time. With exquisite care he ran his hands down her arms to her wrists.

He kissed her fingertips and ordered gruffly, "Listen to me. It doesn't matter whether you've got a wooden leg, a wig, a prosthesis or anything else. What matters is that surgery saved your life, that you're here and, to get downright selfish about it, that you're here with me. The rest is purely extraneous. That settled, we're going dancing," he hurriedly decided as her thigh accidently brushed his hard flesh. "Back to our place, the piano bar."

As C.C. casually moved from her he applauded his wisdom. He wanted desperately to make love to her. Instead he was taking her dancing, like the sensitive man he was, or at least *hoped* he was.

But she didn't want to go dancing. She had a headache, she said, and would really like to go home.

At a loss for what else to say or do to comfort her, he took her home.

At her door she made a small joke that wrenched him. "By the way, C.C., I don't have to wear a wig, so you can stop worrying about that," she said with droll mockery. "My hair, at least, is my own."

He laughed and kissed her nose, feeling helpless, feeling inadequate, feeling wild. Tenderness burned within him.

Before he could come up with a suitable reply, she touched her lips to his cheek and slipped inside the door.

Traces of her perfume lingered in his car, on him, in his living room. Something, the lovely scent, perhaps, made his heart ache. C.C. went to his study and poured a Scotch.

Downing half of it at a swallow, he sat down in his chair and thought about it all, drawing pictures in his mind that kept twisting his guts.

Her breasts were so beautiful, small, but so alluringly full and round. *Breast,* he corrected himself. What did she look like under that silky little dress?

He shrugged; what did it matter? She was still Valerie. The loss of a breast or anything else would never change that.

But some jerk had made her doubt herself, doubt her sexual attractiveness. Well, he thought grimly, that, at least, he could fix.

An hour or so later, clad in white silk pajamas, Valerie stood at her bedroom window watching the moon floating in its shroud of filmy clouds. Tears still stained her high cheekbones and she felt empty and drained. Each time she thought back to tonight's events, something hot and tight squeezed her chest.

She placed her hand there, across the flatness. *It could be altered, become round and full again. With surgery.* She shuddered. She was afraid. It was the same fear that had led her to postpone her reconstructive surgery. Sighing, she sat down on the bed and wiped her eyes. Even the thought of going back under the knife hollowed her stomach with anxiety.

C.C. had said it didn't matter. Was he just kidding himself? She lowered her head, defeated by the lack of an answer. She was glad she'd told him her secret and its accompanying fears. But she didn't know what to think about the outcome of their conversation. He had held her and kissed her, and she had felt the passion trembling his body. His fevered kiss had ignited her own passion, until she, too, was trembling with desire. A strong, fiery desire that had made her willing to take risks, she reminded herself.

But nothing had come of it.

Dully she warned herself not to jump to conclusions. It was possible that her worst fears hadn't happened. Maybe he just needed time to absorb the shock inherent in the very word *cancer*.

Maybe. She didn't know. After all her thinking and analyzing, all she really knew was that she had yielded fully to the beautiful idea of making love with him.

But he wasn't in the mood to love her.

Or just didn't want to.

Or couldn't.

She had no idea which one to believe.

Ten

Valerie and Dempsey the cat walked through the golden light of dawn, down the long patio and across the yard to the circle of soil planted to pansies. Leaning down, she plucked one of the merry-faced blossoms and touched it to her lips. It smelled faintly sweet and moist from the dew that lay thick as frost upon the ground. Memories of last night still burdened her spirit, but the day was lovely, with high, pillowy clouds and a ravishing baby-blue sky, and she couldn't help responding to its beauty. A fine day to walk beside a small lake, she thought with a poignant smile.

"I'll call you tomorrow," he had said as they walked to her door. Now, picking her way back across the damp lawn, she wondered what they would talk about. She felt awkward just imagining seeing him again. But she refused to give into the angered disappointment that ached her throat. He couldn't help feeling whatever he was feeling.

She picked up Dempsey, grimacing as his wet paws printed her robe with little brown circles, and went back inside. With methodical competence, she prepared breakfast—fruit cups, toast, rice with cream and honey—and set it on the table just as her sister came into the kitchen, fresh from the shower.

"So how was your date last night?" Stephanie asked immediately.

Valerie frowned. "Just fine. Eat your breakfast. What's on the agenda today? Anything special?"

"A doctor's appointment. Checkup time," Stephanie said, reluctantly accepting her sister's evasiveness. "There's a bunch of things I really need done this morning: go over a landscaping plan with the Claytons in Champion Forest—no difficulty there, it's all written down. Then check on the crew working in the Woodlands—they'll be finishing up, and since they're new I want to make sure it's done right. Oh, and then deliver C.C.'s revised landscaping plan to his office. He wants showier plants than we had on the original. Can you take care of the Claytons and C.C.? I'll go check on the crew after I'm finished. And don't forget my trip to Houston tonight."

"Yes, of course I'll check on C.C." Lowering her head, Valerie spooned up the hot, sweet rice. Meeting C.C. on the neutral ground of business might not be such a bad idea. But she was nervous about explaining a landscaping plan to the Claytons.

She need not have been. As Stephanie said, there was nothing to it once one understood the whole picture. The Claytons owned a large country-manor-type home, and the proposed landscaping enhanced that concept. Valerie sailed through the presentation with a minimum of unease.

Her confidence buoyed, she drove on to C.C.'s office. The redwood building with its split-rail fence was situated in a grove of tall pines, reached by a path that wound around the front to a side-porch entrance. So this was where he had worked out his grief and anguish, she mused, gazing around her with saddened perspective. She could almost see him coming out this door at night, the proud shoulders slumped under the burden of his sorrows, the lithe frame tense with weariness and the onset of reality.

Shivering, she stepped inside. He wasn't there. She gave the papers to his secretary and quickly left.

An hour or so later, Valerie was sitting in her own office when she heard his husky laugh. The door was open, and she could see him making his way through the crowded shop. Her heart did an alarming little flip-flop as his smile found her face. She stood, her gaze riveted on him. A pulse beat raggedly in her throat. Damn, but he was attractive! Magnetically so, judging by the reaction of feminine personnel and customers alike. Soft, faded jeans stressed his masculine strength. The sleek muscles of his upper torso were sheathed in a red knit pullover shirt. Deeply tanned skin, wind-tousled hair and a boyish grin completed the picture of an infinitely desirable man.

"Hello, Valerie," C.C. said softly.

"C.C.," she said, inclining her head. Rendered graceless by his surprise appearance, she knocked against the side of the desk, sending a stack of pamphlets skidding to the floor. Flushed with self-annoyance, she knelt and began gathering them.

He stepped into the windowless little office and closed the door, an act that was guaranteed to increase the staff's curiosity tenfold, Valerie fumed. She could just imagine the speculation taking place out there!

She sat back on her heels. "C.C., didn't you get my message? I left the plans with your secretary."

"I know. I just wanted to see you. Worth the trip, Val. You look like a sunbeam in that pretty yellow dress." Stooping, he finished gathering the pamphlets and piled them back on the desk. His voice lowered to intimacy. "I also wanted to tell you about tonight. I have some very fine plans for tonight. We're going to have a delicious dinner catered and served on a table beside a crackling fire—"

"It's sixty-five degrees outside."

"It will be forty by this evening. After dinner we'll dance a little, drink champagne, make love in my big, wide bed."

Valerie caught her breath as a sensual thrill spun along her nerves. Not for the first time with this man, she found herself speechless. Was he just kidding around?

"C.C. . . ." She shook her head and tried again. "Sometimes, like now, I don't know what to say, or how to act with you."

"Don't act. Just be yourself."

This is me, she thought. All confused to hell and gone.

"Very well." Her chin went up. "I assume I do have some say in this?"

The corners of his mouth lifted in a tender crook of a smile. "That's yourself, all right," he said wryly. "But, yes, of course you do. I was hoping you liked my plan—sure seemed a fine one to me." He stepped closer. "What part do you object to?"

"I would enjoy having dinner with you."

His eyes darkened momentarily. "I think you'd enjoy it all. But we'll go with dinner right now. I'll pick you up."

"I'd prefer to drive myself if you don't mind."

"Why?"

Because this way I can cut and run if and when I want to. "I'd just prefer driving myself. I'm feeling a little wary, C.C.," she confessed. "What I told you last night changed our relationship to something I'm not comfortable with yet."

"Then we'll get comfortable with it," C.C. declared.

After telling her to be at his house at seven, he left, feeling darned good about himself. But, hell, he'd been a pretty wonderful guy last night. Warm and loving and sensitive to his woman's needs. His woman. He liked that. And he was going to make love to her tonight. Not only because he wanted to with a desperation that jolted him, but because it was also the sensible thing to do. She'd been hurt, her feminine ego dealt a severe blow, and he was going to take her to bed and heal the wounds.

Valerie wondered if nervousness was going to become a way of life. Her hands shook as she slid a satin slip over her bra and the garters that held up the silkiest of hose. Potent little quills of excitement kept racing through her veins, quickening her pulses and trembling her fingers as she worked with her hair. At first she left the freshly washed mane flowing around her shoulders. Then she changed her mind, as she'd done a dozen times tonight, and fashioned a stern French twist. She stepped into a periwinkle-blue wool dress styled with long sleeves and flaring skirt. High-heeled pumps, tiny gold hoop earrings; against all odds she was dressed.

Her mind had worn a track around C.C.'s words spoken earlier in the day. Her bones threatened to liquefy when she thought about his fine plan, but defenses honed to a fine edge countered the threat. He hadn't wanted her last night. Why had he changed his mind? Pity? Maybe doing her a little favor?

She shivered. "Don't be silly, Valerie," she admonished herself out loud. "It takes more than pity to arouse a man." At least she hoped so.

She checked her appearance three times and still wasn't satisfied. "You are forty years old," she reminded herself, which resolved nothing. She felt sixteen. Thankfully she didn't have Stephanie's sweet curiosity to contend with tonight. Her sister had gone into Houston with some friends.

Valerie put on a warm wool cloak and gloves. As C.C. predicted, a blue norther had blown in and the temperature hovered right at forty degrees when she walked out to her car. Opening her slim black purse, she took out the glasses necessary for driving. C.C. didn't even know she was near-sighted. Did he need glasses? She hadn't seen him wear any, except for sunglasses. But she hadn't seen him reading, ei-ther. He probably needed them then... She gave an ironic little laugh. What a petty thing to be fretting about!

She drove slowly, both eager and reluctant to see him. A black caterer's van was parked in the drive. She pulled in beside it. C.C. opened the beautiful French doors at the side of the house and she fairly flew in, propelled by the wind ballooning her cape. Laughing, he caught and steadied her.

"Rotten night!" she said.

"Lovely night," C.C. corrected. Impulsively he kissed her hand, then took a white rose from the foyer arrangement and gave it to her. He felt overpoweringly romantic and his cheeks burned as he glanced toward the living room. But his gesture hadn't been noticed. And what was there to notice? he demanded of himself. He had simply kissed a woman's hand and given her a rose. Nothing so outrageous about that, he thought a trifle defensively. His blood raced as she slipped out of her wrap. With her hair up and those dark eyes outlined with kohl, she looked beguiling, mysterious. Her clingy dress revealed the contours of her body with every move she made.

Sensing his excitement and pleased by it as well as by his gallant gesture, Valerie turned her attention to the activity taking place in the living room. Two black-clad waiters were arranging a small table in front of the fireplace, where a cheery fire snapped and crackled its delight in the wind. The napery was crisp white linen, set with C.C.'s fine china, crystal and silver. Champagne chilled in a gilt cooler. The centerpiece was pale pink lilies and three pink candles, which were quickly lit and the lights dimmed.

Two small silver compotes holding shrimp cocktails were placed on the table. "Madame," one of the waiters said, pulling out her chair with a courteous bow.

Valerie was feeling a little dazzled by the pleasure of it all. She allowed herself to be seated with a gleeful smile shared with C.C., who seemed to be getting as big a kick out of this as she was.

"Glad you came?" he asked with a smug grin.

Valerie touched her lips with a napkin, noting, with a secret thrill, how closely he watched, as if fascinated by the small gesture. "Yes, of course I am. I love to be pampered," she confessed.

Dinner was marvelous, a salad of tender young lettuces and hothouse cherry tomatoes, grilled lobster with drawn butter, asparagus and flaky rolls, served with champagne in flutes so thin and delicate that Valerie feared a careless grip would snap the long stem.

Dessert was a palate-cleansing sherbet. Afterward they moved to easy chairs to enjoy the silky fullness of champagne while the waiters discreetly cleared the table, and just as discreetly departed.

The centerpiece was left on the table, candles still burning, lights still dim. From somewhere in the room came the liquid notes of a slow, plaintive melody. A stereo on a timer, she supposed, her breath catching as C.C. stood and held out his arms to her.

"We can enjoy the second part of my plan, can't we?" he asked when she hesitated.

The seductive note in his voice set her pulses racing. "Yes," she replied huskily. "I guess we can."

Valerie went into his embrace with what she considered unseemly eagerness. His smooth-shaven cheek came against hers and the contact was unbearably sweet. She moved dreamily to the music, lulled by sensuous rhythms and the undemanding warmth of his arms.

Then it all changed. His clasp tightened. His mustache made a slow, sensuous trail down her cheek. Her mouth caught his, and clung. He slid his hands down her back and gently pulled her against him. She was acutely aware of the imprint of his firm, inflexible thighs. The tight peak of her breast pressed into his thin shirt as if seeking more intimate warmth.

Unsettled by her swift, hot response to his masculinity, she drew back and looked up at him. "And what about the third part of your plan? What made you decide to make love to me? Noblesse oblige?" she asked with sardonic humor.

He looked bewildered.

She glanced away. "Last night you didn't want to, tonight you do. Why? Boy Scout generosity—doing your good deed for the day?" She spoke lightly, almost playfully, and C.C.'s swift reaction startled her.

"Good deed?" he exclaimed incredulously. Then he swore, dangerously soft and low. An instant later his mouth swooped down on hers, cutting across her protest, silencing thought and reason with hard, raging kisses.

Senses reeling under his delicious onslaught, Valerie grabbed at his shoulders and just held on. She was being ravished with kisses! It delighted her. It frightened her. She made no conscious decision; she was simply swept along on a rushing, pulsing wave of desire so intense she did not even try to resist its demands. Threading her fingers into his hair, she kissed him with that lovely, burning need that blotted out logic.

A hot shout of exultation exploded in her blood as he groaned and caught her tighter. His mouth was enchantingly rough and hungry. Hands gone wild with passion strained her closer, pressing deeper, harder, until her wantonly pliant curves fused to his taut planes. A similar exultance echoed through her mind. There was no mistaking his passion. He wanted her as much as she wanted him!

But did he need her as much? Irritably she thrust the orphan thought aside and concentrated on the sensuous flux of sensations. Sensations and emotions she had forgotten existed, feelings and needs too long denied. A shiver trembled the length of her body. He muttered her name, questioningly.

"Wonderful," she half moaned. "So wonderful, the way you feel to me, the way you taste."

Her husky words excited him more. With a beguiling lack of effort, he swept her up and carried her to his bedroom.

When he put her down and reached for the light, Valerie stayed his hand. "No, C.C. Please."

"Yes, Val. I want to see you, darling," he coaxed huskily.

Caught up in doubt, she was slow to release his hand. She stood perfectly still while C.C. walked to the bedroom's white-marbled fireplace and lit the three tall ivory candles that graced the mantel. Two he left there, one he carried to his night table.

"Okay?"

"Okay."

While he watched with rapt intensity, she stepped out of her dress and laid it on his valet chair. He sucked in his breath as the satin slip fell in a shimmering circle about her feet.

"No, let me," he said when she began unfastening her stockings. With obvious pleasure, he finished disrobing her, except for the lacy black bra. When he reached for the fastener, something stirred at the back of her mind and she stopped him.

"No," she said sharply.

"Val, come on now, this is me, remember?" he reminded. "You have nothing to fear from me."

"I know, but I...please, C.C., I don't want to take it off just yet." She stared at him, at the tightening mouth, the dark lashes feathering his rugged cheekbones. "Please," she repeated softly.

C.C. blew out his breath. He'd already made one bad mistake in judgment. He couldn't afford another. "All right, not just yet, honey. But soon. You're so beautiful, Valerie. I don't want you hiding anything about that lovely body from me. Here, let me take down your hair, baby. This excites me, you know," he whispered as the silken fall spilled down over his hands. •

Stepping away from her, he swiftly undressed, his gaze fastened on her glowing dusk-and-ivory beauty. When he turned back to her, the magnificence of his aroused body took her breath.

"Come here," he huskily commanded. Valerie obeyed with that same wanton eagerness. He wrapped his arms around her and buried his face in her hair. For a time he just held her, creating such a soft, sensuous intimacy that she lost her breath again. She felt his heart beating against hers, felt the sexual tension in iron-muscled arms that threatened to crush her slender fragility into hard, male flesh and bone. The potent sensation of naked skin against naked skin sent jolt after jolt of excitement coursing through her. Mindlessly she sought his mouth.

A blaze of kisses raced from her face to her shoulders, sliding down to the top of her bra and back up again, seeking out the satin curve of her neck and chin, the fragrant spot behind her ear. She loved the cool, velvety whisk of his mustache on her hot skin. His hand trailed downward and found the mound of softness that ached to take him in. With a passionate moan she arched against him. She could wait no longer for the fulfillment of union with him. Whispering his name, she moved her hips in a rhythmic invitation as ancient as time itself.

They sank down on the bed, bodies fused together in wild and glorious need. Wet and hungry, his mouth caught hers again, while his hands explored with fevered urgency. Shifting, a movement that made both of them moan with rapturous frustration, she guided his fingers beneath her bra to the breast that ached for his touch. Pleasure shivered through her as his fingertips found the hard little peak. But he kept his mouth on hers.

She ran her hands over his smooth skin, lightly, maddeningly, and felt his shudder, heard him groan. The need to be filled with him was a kind of delirium of the senses. Moaning, she tangled her hands in his hair and tugged, thrilling to the demanding weight of him, loving the wide breadth of shoulders, the lean, taut body stretching to cover hers.

"C.C., I need you." She gasped against his devouring mouth. "Now. Now."

Dimly she heard his low, triumphant laugh. A moment later he came to her with a splendor that blotted out the world.

It seemed incredibly natural to wake up in C. C. Wyatt's arms. Opening her eyes, Valerie felt only the smallest trace of disorientation and that disappeared the instant she became aware of the leg he had thrown across her hip.

The candles had burned themselves out, giving the room over to moonlight shining in the arched window high above the bed. Turning her head, she gazed at him yearningly. In the mellow light coming from the hallway, his face looked young and vulnerable with its softened planes and the dusky lashes shadowing his cheeks. But there was nothing soft about the jawline she traced with a butterfly touch of fingertip. He stirred, then stilled again. The deep breath she drew was filled with the delicious mix of scents that accompanied their intimacy. A joyous little shiver ran along her skin. It had been so long since she'd experienced the incomparable pleasure of being loved, and loved well, the euphoric aftermath that led to blissful slumber. Greedily, she wanted more of it.

And there was the danger, she thought sadly, the ever-present danger. She could get addicted to this man. She could get badly hurt. And she'd already had so much heartache. But she could also have a lot of pleasure...

Choices again. Decisions. She couldn't make one, not in this haze of confusion. No longer sleepy, she wriggled, but she was held captive by an arm around her midriff and the leg across her hip. Carefully she slid sideways from beneath his imprisoning limbs and stood.

A hand caught her arm. When C.C. came awake, he came wide-awake. "Valerie? Where you going, honey?" he asked clearly.

"Home. No, now lie still, C.C."

"I'll see you home, if you must go," he said, sitting up.

"Oh, don't be ridiculous, I can see my own self home," she stated. "And don't frown at me, there's nothing wrong with a woman leaving a man for a change, rather than vice versa."

He lay back against the pillows and studied her. "There's not, hmm?"

"No, there's not." She found her slip and hastily put it on. "Oh, don't turn on the light, C.C.!" she protested the soft glare of lamplight. "I'm all wrinkled and rumpled!"

"Deliciously wrinkled and rumpled," he agreed.

Valerie sighed. She stood beside the bed, and his gaze was lusty upon her body. His mouth had that hungry look again. She could feel things beginning to heat up and she wasn't sure she wanted that.

"C.C.," she said warningly, but that was as far as she got. Two big hands encircled her waist and dragged her down atop him in a flurry of limbs and satin skirts.

His quick, fluid movement brought her beneath him.
Desire spilled through her like a wave of effervescent heat.
His husky voice plied her senses, his hands moved over her
with those rough-gentle caresses so intoxicating in their
fevered passion. Giving up any thought of escape, she tangled her fingers in his hair and matched his hard hunger with
her own.

An immeasurable time later, she wanted to float into sleep
again, but it would be dawn soon and God forbid that she
confront Stephanie looking like this. "Let me up, C.C.,"
she demanded somewhat petulantly. "You're heavy. And I
have to go."

"Go where?" came his drowsy voice from the depths of
her hair.

"Well, to the bathroom first, then home. Do you want me
walking out of here in broad daylight?"

He raised his head. "Wouldn't bother me."

"Well, it would me."

"Seriously?"

"Yes, seriously."

He rolled from her and propped up on an elbow. Hook-
ing a finger beneath her bra, he asked, "When are we taking this off?"

"I don't know, C.C." She pulled away and sat up. "Just
don't harass me about it, all right?"

"All right." His gaze captured hers. "Then I am seeing
you again?"

She hesitated. Then, almost imperceptibly, her slim white
shoulders sagged. "Yes, of course. Did you doubt it?"

"Yes, I doubted it. I don't take anything about you for
granted," he muttered, and she laughed.

"You better not." On impulse, she leaned down and
kissed him. Then, softly, "Thank you, C.C."

"Thank me!" he echoed. "What on earth for?"

"For loving me tonight, for showing me that I'm still sexually attractive."

"Oh, Valerie, for God's sake," he growled. "You're one of the loveliest, most desirable women I've ever known. I don't see how you could lose track of that."

"I've had a hard climb up from a very deep well, C.C. I'm not quite there yet," she said quietly.

"I know it's been hard, baby. But it's over now." A fingertip tilted up her chin. "Is that why all that stuff about noblesse oblige and good deeds?" he asked testily.

"Yes. I thought perhaps you might have something to prove, too. Your words," she explained as he lifted an eyebrow.

He grunted. "The only thing I had to prove was that I wasn't going to die if I didn't get you into my bed, and I was having a bit of trouble doing that." He studied her: the faint smile his words evoked, the silken tumble of her hair falling around her face and shoulders, the beauty of ivory satin against her skin. "Last night was a mistake in judgment on my part, nothing more. So no more of that garbage, you hear?"

"I hear," Valerie said. She just wished she believed it.

Eleven

―――

"Another date with C.C.?" Stephanie inquired as her sister walked into the room wearing a chic black dress, pearls and high heels. "This is the fourth one this week. We can say you're dating now, can't we?"

Valerie sighed. "Yes, they're dates, Stephanie."

Stephanie tilted her head. "Why are you so loathe to admit that?"

"I guess because I'm human and a female," Valerie answered lightly. "I don't want to get my little heart broken."

"C.C. wouldn't break your heart! I'd tear him apart with my bare hands if he dared hurt you," the younger woman declared.

"Thank you, love, that makes me feel heaps better," Valerie drawled. "Anyway, I do have another date with him tonight, and possibly every night until I go home. Except for tomorrow night, of course. Then it's your turn."

"I still don't see why I have to go to that banquet with you two tomorrow night. What am I, a decoy?"

"Exactly. Photographers never pay attention to me when you're around." The old clock in the hall chimed the hour and Valerie checked her watch against it. C.C. would be here in five minutes. That, if nothing else, she could count on.

Turning to a framed mirror, she set a small black hat atop her head and tilted the veil downward until it touched her nose. A glance into quizzical green eyes provoked a frown. "Steffie, I told you, I just hate the thought of being the object of speculation."

"And I don't?" her sister inquired with a toss of her head.

"No, but you're used to it," Valerie said with a puckish smile. "I'm not."

"I don't see how that counts for anything. Where are you going tonight?"

"To the symphony. Another side of C.C. I didn't expect. The man has so many facets I have a hard time keeping up with him," Valerie confessed delightedly.

Stephanie whistled. "How'd he get tickets? That concert's been sold out for weeks."

"Evidently he persuaded someone to part with theirs." Valerie pulled on black elbow-length gloves. "C.C. can be quite persuasive," she murmured. A quivery sensation shook her as she visualized where the evening would end. In his bed, in a glorious tumble of love.

Lovemaking, she corrected. No words of love had been spoken. Nor was she expecting any. She didn't even know her own feelings yet. Her emotions were too snarled in confusion and fluttery fears to sort out, even had she made the effort. Which she hadn't. Who knew what she'd discover at the center of that confusion? Self-preservation decreed that she proceed with care.

Stephanie chose that moment to say, "Well, with all these dates, it strikes me that I ought to seriously consider adding C.C. to my list of 'wedding march' candidates!"

Valerie glanced away, her features suddenly sharp and drawn. "Hey, lay off that, will you? Some things aren't funny, Stephanie."

Startled, Stephanie bit down on her lip. "Oh, Val, I'm sorry," she said confusedly.

Contrarily, Valerie laughed. "Now why are you sorry?" she chided. "Because you don't think he'd want me?"

"No, I'd never think that. He'd be lucky to get you, Val, you know that," Stephanie said fiercely.

"Well, I like to think so," Valerie drawled, but she felt too soft and happy, more in the mood to share than to bristle. She ruffled her sister's hair. "Oh, stop looking so dismayed, honey. You just scratched a fantasy, that's all. I mean, the man *is* the best-looking thing I've seen this side of the Mississippi!" She began to laugh. "But it's rather like pairing Mother Goose with Prince Charming—it boggles the mind, particularly when there are two little goslings traipsing along behind!"

"Huh. If the man doesn't realize the value of a complete package, then he's not worthy of the name," Stephanie declared. She tilted her head again. "I could get out my shotgun."

"Thanks, but no thanks. Let's just table this discussion, shall we? Permanently," Valerie said, already regretting the conversation. Fantasies were private business. Besides, this one had just popped up from some hazy nowhere. And it didn't help to realize that she was falling in love with C. C. Wyatt. She drew a tremulous breath, followed by a deeper one, before speaking again. "What do you think of this outfit?"

"Gorgeous. I don't know anyone else who could carry off a hat like that. I love it!"

"Thank you. I just hope C.C. loves it, too," Valerie fretted.

C.C. did. Admiringly he studied her.

"You sure you want to go out with me? You look like you should be on the arm of one of those Armani types instead of mine," he drawled.

"I think I am on the arm of one of those Armani types," she replied with a measuring glance at his superbly tailored suit. He laughed, but it didn't reach his eyes. Wondering what was bothering him, she handed him her cloak.

Her pleasure in the symphony was dimmed by his faintly distracted manner. Impulsively she slipped her hand into his and they sat like that, their shoulders touching. Her new and deep-seated need to be touched alarmed her even while she enjoyed it.

After the concert they stopped by his private club for liqueurs. In the dim-lit room with its soft music, she felt intimately attuned to him. When he leaned to speak to her, she turned her head, and he rested his lips at the corner of hers to bedevil both their senses. Under the table his hand drifted across her stomach. "Let's go home," he suggested huskily.

Except for that hint of remoteness that surfaced when conversation lapsed, C.C. was his usual charming self on the drive home. She waited until they had reached his house to inquire, "C.C., is anything wrong? You seemed somewhat distracted this evening."

C.C. finished hanging up her coat and turned to her with a husky laugh. "My mind was on this," he murmured, pulling her into his arms. He brushed his mustache across her upper lip for a sensual thrill before catching her mouth in a long, soft kiss. Desire came gently, like an extra coat of warmth glossing her body. His mouth slanted across hers, teasing, persuading, so sweet she wanted more and more.

His lean thighs came hard against hers and she gasped with pleasure. The current of passion engulfed her, still gentle, still so softly persuasive that it was unthinkable not to go with it. She made a little sound of disappointment when he removed his lips from hers. But he assuaged it by taking her hand and walking with her to the bedroom.

He removed the sexy little hat and took down her hair, nibbled her earlobe. She pulled away and turned her back. "Unzip me, please?"

He obeyed, then kissed the pearly flesh revealed by parting fabric. Beneath the dress she wore a red bra, and panties cut high on the thigh.

"Those long, gorgeous legs," he said with a lusty sigh. Her hose were held up with ruffled garters. "I'm so damn glad you don't wear panty hose," he said.

"I do, for practical purposes."

She laughed as he eagerly removed the garters. But she took off the filmy hose herself, sitting down on the bed and rolling them neatly downward while he watched, entranced.

She helped him undress, taking pleasure in the lovely business of ridding him of shirt and tie. There she stopped, and slid into bed to watch him finish disrobing. Her gaze ranged down the long male frame, all power and thrust and potent force. She felt heady with the desire flooding the secret places of her body.

C.C.'s breath suspended as he turned and looked at her. Her hair lay dark and lush against the creamy pillow. Her eyes were glazed with the passion flushing her creamy skin, her lips parted in tempting invitation. He got into bed beside her and captured them in a hard, possessive kiss.

Then, abruptly breaking the luscious contact, he raised his head and looked at her. The question that had plagued him all evening was quickly and resolutely decided. His hands slid across her neck to the bra's clasp. "Val, let's take this off now. I don't like it between us, either how it feels or what it signifies.''

Panic flashed in her eyes, but she asked coolly, ''What does it signify?''

''A lack of trust in me. Now stop wriggling so I can unfasten this thing.''

''No! C.C., don't,'' she ordered, trying to get away from his clever fingers. ''This has nothing to do with trust, it's my own personal feelings, that's all. Please, C.C., wait.''

He laid his chin in the center of her bra. ''I'm waiting.''

Valerie fought down panic at the thought of exposing herself to those keen blue eyes. What if he found her ugly? What if he didn't want her after he'd seen her? It mattered so much, so frighteningly much. She was in love with him, she couldn't deny it any longer, and seeing revulsion in those beautiful eyes would surely crush her.

And what if he couldn't perform? If the sight of her destroyed his desire—*turned him off,* she acidly mocked the words of another man—God, she couldn't even bear imagining it!

Impatiently, he shifted. ''Enough, Valerie. This is getting ridiculous.''

''It's not ridiculous. It's…you're just my lover, C.C., not my husband!'' she cried, confused and angry. ''I'll decide when and if I want to take it off, not you.''

Blue eyes glinted. ''Just your lover?''

''No, not just—oh, you *know* what I mean!'' Valerie drew a deep breath. ''C.C. you have an image of me right now that deviates immensely from the real one. I want you to keep that image.''

''My image of you will remain the same, whatever happens,'' he stated. ''Now hold still. This thing's hard enough to do without you trying to escape.''

''Very well,'' she said, but she stiffened despite her efforts to cooperate. A hollow lurch in her belly snarled her breath with the anxious rush of thoughts. She hated that it mattered so much. But it did, and she had to prepare herself. But what *would* he think when he saw her? Would that smile be wiped from his face? If so, replaced with what? Shock? Probably. Revulsion? Possibly. Or worst of all, pity? God! She couldn't stand pity from anyone, but especially not from him!

Inwardly shuddering, Valerie drew a quick breath and grabbed his arm. "But with the light out, C.C."

Feeling the quick, resentful stir of his body, she added hastily, "Please, indulge me? This is very difficult for me. It's not just feminine vanity. Just being with you like this hasn't been easy. Let me take this step by step. Maybe it does seem ridiculous to you," she went on a little stiffly, "but I need it to be this way. Please turn out the light."

"Oh, Val." C.C. sighed. But he yielded to her plea and snapped off the bedside lamp.

Once unfastened, the prosthetic bra was quickly discarded. Valerie lay quietly accepting his gentle explorations. His touch on her breast was a lovely, tingling sensation, rousing her nipple to tautness within seconds. But there was no pleasure in his touch on the empty place beside it. She waited while he placed a series of kisses on the benumbed area.

A tremulous breath escaped her when he put his mouth to her breast. Wonderful, this tugging of teeth and lips! When callused fingertips moved down her stomach, she turned her face and his mouth slid across hers, firm and hot and exciting. Eyes closed, she felt him shift, felt the sweet, velvety torment of his mustache moving down her sensitive skin, setting her nerve endings afire with the most delicious sensations.

Enraptured, she released the last of her tension and gave herself up to delight. It was so right, all so beautifully right, she thought just before she forgot how to think.

* * *

C.C. shifted in his chair, enough so that his thigh brushed against Valerie's. The banquet they were attending was incredibly boring, or would have been had she not been there with him. Speeches were being made, awards given out. He didn't receive any, but then he had three already, for excellence of design of homes in various price ranges, a fact he managed to make certain she knew without sounding like a braggart.

It wasn't all that important a fact. But it seemed important that she know it.

He glanced at her, liking the soft lines of ivory silk on her slender shoulders and back. Stephanie sat on the other side of him, lovely in a fine, yellow wool tunic over a long taupe skirt. He felt ten feet tall sandwiched between his beautiful women. At least they were thought to be his. Later he would have to disabuse his acquaintances of this fanciful notion by introducing Valerie as Stephanie's sister and partner. But for right now, well, he was only human and very much a man. He'd be less than both if he didn't experience at least a twinge of enjoyment from his imagined position.

Although the interest that people took in his sex life both perplexed and amused him, he couldn't really blame Valerie for her reluctance to be thought of as his "latest." So maybe it was better that their estimation of him and Stephanie remain the same. At least they wouldn't degrade Stephanie by thinking he'd gone from her to her sister.

He shuddered. What an ugly thought. And how inextricably entangled he was with these two women. He hadn't realized that until now.

He felt a little odd about that, like a plant captured by a flowerpot, C.C. thought wryly. He leaned nearer as if to speak to Valerie, and the fragrance of perfumed bath oils on satiny female flesh enveloped his senses. He tuned out the speechmaking and thought about the silk and lace she wore against her skin. His mind remembered vividly how she had looked in his bed last night. From there his charged recall flew to the moment he had touched her chest and felt the stunning comparison of the full, rounded globe of one breast and the jarring absence of the other. His heart had been wrenched. It still hurt.

Under the table, his fingers enlaced with hers. He projected his thoughts forward, to the end of the evening, and felt a sharp pang of resentment. Intuitively he knew that she would not be sharing his bed tonight. She'd go inside with Stephanie, and that would be that. Not so much as a goodnight kiss, he'd bet. She had an endearing streak of modesty in her, along with an obdurate sense of what was right and proper.

The speeches stopped. Music began to play. People were rising, mingling, making their leisurely way to the wine and food tables at the back of the room, or, as in Stephanie and Valerie's case, to the powder room.

He kept a sharp eye out for their return. Stephanie stopped to greet someone and to introduce her sister. Then they wandered on. But everywhere Valerie went in the huge banquet hall, she was his focal point.

He had feared getting involved with her, now he feared the depth of involvement. He wasn't a masochist. He didn't want to get hurt again, that dreadful kind of hurt that knew no solace...

Irritably he chopped off that line of thought. He was in full control of himself. In no danger, he assured himself. But, oh, he did like this bright, lovely woman! That part of it, he admitted gingerly, was immune to discipline.

During the drive home she and Stephanie got to talking about the nearness of Christmas. "Only eighteen more shopping days left, and I haven't even begun!" Valerie sighed. "You are going to come and spend Christmas with us, aren't you, Steffie?"

After considering it, Stephanie decided she was.

C.C. felt a pinch somewhere in his chest as he thought about his past Christmases. Jordan was going skiing, so this one wouldn't be any different. Just lonelier.

"When are you leaving?" he asked quietly. He hadn't really thought about her leaving again and it jolted him.

"The tenth. I've so much to do, packing and all," Valerie said vaguely.

Three more days with her. Another reason to resent going home alone tonight, C.C. thought irritably. They had things to settle between them, and he was impatient to get started.

Instead he had to watch her stroll up the walk with Stephanie, and the door shutting him out.

Two nights later, Valerie glided around C.C.'s bedroom with silken assurance. They'd had dinner in a cozy little restaurant, then gone dancing. They had danced the delicious way lovers do, soft and slow and bonelessly close, a tantalizing prelude to lovemaking.

She felt now as she did then, languorous, sexy, desirable. Clad in her slip and bra, her hair flowing around her shoulders, she turned down the bed with trembling fingers. C.C. appeared resigned to making love with the lights off, and she anticipated a rapturous, problem-free evening.

Shirtless, he watched her with a quizzical little smile. She met his blue gaze and felt a deep inner softening. With feminine delight she stopped before him and traced the golden line of hair down his flat belly to the waistband of his trousers.

Bemused and beguiled, C.C. watched those slim, moving fingers with rapt attention. The beating within him matched the rhythm of the pulse throbbing in her throat. He stopped her hands and stripped off her slip. She looked so exciting in that little scrap of fabric and lace that cupped her bosom. But he wanted it off. Not just because it challenged him, but because he honestly feared she was using her self-doubts to build a barrier between them.

Whether she was doing so consciously or unconsciously, he didn't know. His suspicions were still vague, composed mostly of dread of losing her. But he thought she was creating a wall around herself with her mistrust of him, a safe place where he couldn't enter, and the heart-twisting disturbance he felt was very real. She could use that barrier to harden her heart, to the point of walking away from him rather than risk possible rejection.

Of course he wouldn't be repelled, but she didn't know that. And he couldn't think of any way to let her know. Except to *show* her—

She interrupted his thoughts by unfastening his trousers.

C.C. stood stock-still as she began pulling them down his legs. He seemed to have no will of his own, he noticed distractedly. Being totally undressed by her was utterly disarming. When she'd finished, she sat him on the bed and removed his socks. She tossed them aside and pulled him back up to her with a breathless little laugh.

His laugh was a trifle breathless, too. He was naked, and she had done it. Done it with those cool, slender fingers, fingers that moved from his shoulders to his hips in a long, hungry glide. A rush of desire shot through him, making him almost dizzy with its fiery demands.

He snapped out the light. Then, with an exultant laugh, he tumbled her down on the bed and gave up thinking altogether.

After the glory came the wonder of holding her to his heart while savoring the voluptuous languor that was such a vital part of their lovemaking. Gradually they settled into comfortable positions, bodies touching, faces close.

"When will you be back?" he asked drowsily.

"The week after Christmas." She curled her fingers on his chest. "So that the girls can have a little visit, see their new home... will you miss me?"

"I suppose I will," he said. He wished he knew how she felt about him. But he was loath to ask. He might not like what he heard, and he didn't want anything to spoil the joy of what they shared.

At some point in the lovely dark, she got up to go to the bathroom. He supposed he shouldn't have begun it so abruptly. He supposed he should have waited until later, when she was back in bed, held tight in his arms. But if he had one rogue fault, it was impatience, C.C. admitted.

When he heard her returning to the bed, he reached out and turned on the light.

An instant later he regretted it bitterly. She stood like a deer trapped in the glare of headlights. Then she gasped and flung her hands protectively across her chest. Her white face swung up to meet his wary gaze with a blaze of fury.

"How dare you! How dare you just turn on the light like that, catching me like this—how bloody double *dare* you! You insensitive—clod!" she cried, half strangling on her words.

C.C. inwardly shrank from the glare of her dark eyes. "Val, I'm sorry, I wasn't thinking."

"No, you weren't!" Valerie hurled back. The only lucid emotion she could distinguish from the storm in her heart was an intense disappointment in him, centering her fury like the eye of a hurricane. Besides trampling on her needs, he had shattered several of the lovely illusions she'd created around him. "I asked you to wait. I tried to tell you how important it was to me to do this at my own pace—damn it, I *told* you! But, no, you had to take matters into your own hands, had to force the issue."

Her wretched battle with tears imparted a brilliance to her eyes and trembled her mouth as she stared at him.

C.C. threw out his hands, palms up. "Valerie, yes, I did take matters into my own hands, I admit everything you've said. But let me tell you why I did it."

"I know why you did it, because I was being *ridiculous!*" she cut in angrily. "Well, now that you've overcome that little fault of mine—" she flung out her arms. "—what do you think of the results?"

"Ah, my God," C.C. groaned as a mental fist slammed into his solar plexus. Needing desperately to first consider her feelings, he found himself in an equally desperate struggle with his own. He felt a wild mixture of emotions, felt savagely tender, savagely in need of revenge against something or someone, outraged to the point of clenching his fists to keep a grip on himself. His heart cried out at what had been done to her.

He reached for her, blindly needing to comfort her terrible distress, but where were the words, where were the blasted *words!*

"Valerie, it's okay—"

"It's not okay!" She lashed out, shoving him away. Wheeling, she snatched her bra and dress and ran to the bathroom.

C.C. pulled on his trousers and walked around rubbing the back of his neck. The picture of her dear and precious body mutilated like that kept shaking him with brutal hands. He was glad—and maybe secretly relieved, because he was only human—to know that he'd been right on one thing. His desire for her was as strong as ever. Maybe stronger, since he felt this quite savage need to protect her. Well, when she came out, they'd talk and he would try to make known his feelings.

She emerged fully dressed, her hair up, albeit unsteadily. Avoiding his eyes, she stuffed her panties and hose into her pocket. She'd driven over to his house tonight—another one of her little quirks, and it was clear that she had every intention of going straight home.

He stepped toward her. "Valerie, please, let's sit down and talk, honey. I'm not all to blame for this. You know I've been patient with you—"

"*Patient* with me!"

"Yes, patient," he plowed doggedly on. "But I am sorry that I pushed you into this."

"So am I." She headed for the living room.

"Val, damn it, wait a minute," he demanded. But now he felt guilty, too, and why wouldn't she listen to reason for once! At least give him a chance to explain his behavior. Then she'd see he was acting in her best interest.

He followed her swiftly moving figure to the foyer. "Val, hey, look, I've apologized, okay? I'm sorry, maybe I was wrong to turn on the light—"

Her mouth twisted. "Maybe?"

"All right, in the strictest sense, I was, but I had a good reason."

"I'm sure you thought you did," Valerie replied, relenting a little. She slipped on her pumps. "but the fact is, there is no good reason to be had. You behaved like an arrogant, insensitive, manipulative male. And I can't abide such as that."

"I'm neither arrogant nor manipulative," C.C. denied. The slow burn of anger sharpened his voice. "Maybe I'm a little insensitive, but I thought I was doing the right thing, Val, showing you, rather than trying to tell you, that I meant every word I said to you. This changes nothing between us, don't you see? You're just as beautiful as ever to me."

"It changes everything between us," she flared, ignoring the last part of his statement. Then she sighed, her shoulders hunching. "Look, C.C., I'm not thinking too clearly right now. I'm angry and confused, and I just want to go home."

"All right," C.C. gave in, since he didn't have any other choice but to physically restrain her. "We'll talk later. But I'll see you home."

"No, now don't start that again," she said wearily. "I'll drive myself home." Opening the closet door, she took out her cloak and threw it over her shoulders. "Good night, C.C.," she said, and left him standing there in the rags of his anger.

Twelve

Valerie packed the way she had learned to do anything else unpleasant, methodically, applying only a tiny thinking part of her mind to the task. She didn't pack much, there were plenty of clothes hanging in her closet at home, and right now she didn't give a fig about clothes.

She zipped up the small bag and set it beside the bedroom door, then stripped off her gown and took a quick shower.

Toweling off was done with no thought for the act. Her mind was preoccupied with C. C. Wyatt. She had decided to leave today instead of tomorrow. Seeing C.C. again this soon was not at the top of her priority list, she thought, grimacing.

Dispassionately she studied herself in the mirror. Her eyes were swollen and red with the tears she had cried last night. Acknowledging how deeply she loved him was cause for another saltwater shower. She had wept until there were no tears left, and then she'd wept some more.

Although she hated admitting it, everything in her had secretly begged and pleaded for some word of affection from him. Anything. A simple "I care" would have sufficed. Well, that she'd fallen in love with a man who could not reciprocate was her tough luck. She could hardly blame him. Like he said, love was either there or it wasn't.

A sensible rationale. But every time she thought of last night's scene, anger gripped her, a bright flame encircling the bitterest-tasting disappointment she'd ever known. She had begun to trust C.C., had come very close to voluntarily placing herself at enormous risk. She had thought him a perceptive, tolerant man, patient with her fears and apprehensions. Her painful fury blazed anew. How could he have been so insensitive, so blind to her needs! To pull a stunt like that—to turn on the light and catch her like an animal in a trap!

She shuddered. It had been embarrassing, humiliating and a shocking intrusion on terribly personal privacy. He had also usurped her right to decide when to take the next step in their relationship, Valerie reminded herself with flinty resolve.

But disillusionment was still strong enough to sting her aching eyes. She felt outraged and hurt, the kind of hurt that would take a long time to heal. Well, her sister had been forced to face a painful truth concerning the man she had loved, and had done so without whimpering. Stephanie had accepted, endured and moved on with her life. A fine example to follow, Valerie told herself sternly. And she would. Beginning now.

All that weeping had accomplished something besides reddening her eyes, she thought wryly. It had drained her of the grief of loss, and washed away the paralysis of fear. She didn't know what the future held in store, but she felt stronger now and capable of facing whatever came her way. And whether or not C.C. remained in her life, she was going to have reconstructive surgery. Not for him, not for any man. For herself. There was simply no sense in walking around feeling so incomplete.

She was still scared, Valerie admitted. In fact, the prospect of going under the knife again knotted up her stomach. But somewhere along the way she had gained control of her fear, not the other way around.

She still hurt, too. Valerie drew a tremulous breath as her thoughts returned to C.C. What had he felt last night?

Irritably she dragged a brush through her hair. This was getting her nowhere. She'd spent futile hours last night trying to distinguish between the emotions streaking through those keen blue eyes! Except for shock, his true feelings were still a mystery to her, but she fancied she'd seen enough to reinforce her decision to return to her Mississippi home as soon as possible.

Give them both time to reflect, she mused, gathering up her hair. Not that she thought that would do much good. It was ruined between them, and he would probably appreciate her decision to leave.

Just the same, she couldn't actually go without saying goodbye. It wasn't proper. Steeling herself, she dialed his office. But he'd gone out to the Parade of Homes site, the secretary said. Any message?

"Just tell him I've decided to leave for the holidays. And please wish him Merry Christmas for me?"

Putting down the telephone, she went back to her dressing table and patted concealing makeup around her eyes. She still had to say goodbye to her sister. Stephanie had gone on to work this morning, leaving her sleeping.

She was outside when Valerie arrived at the nursery, her bright hair shining like a beacon in the sunlight. Zipping her jacket, for there was a brisk wind blowing, Valerie approached her with a loving smile.

"How pretty you are!" she said, kissing her sister's cheek. "Can we talk, honey? I'm leaving in a few minutes for Mississippi and I wanted to say goodbye."

Stephanie's face clouded. "A day early? Any particular reason?"

"A lot of things crowding in on me. Goodness, I still have cards to address, presents to buy and wrap. I'm going to need every minute between now and Christmas!" Valerie said gaily.

"Okay..." Sea-green eyes flashed up to hers. "But what about C.C.? I mean, you were dating and all."

"C.C.'s fine to have as a friend," Valerie said carefully. "But as a man, he's not quite what I thought he was. Or perhaps just wanted him to be."

Stephanie gave her a pained look. "Oh, Val, I know he's not a gallant white knight, but he's a decent guy. At least I thought so."

"Yes, of course he is. But I...well, let's just say I wanted qualities he doesn't seem to possess, and let it go at that. Luckily we didn't get serious," Valerie said brightly. "Don't worry about me, okay? Bye, honey, see you at Christmas."

"I can't wait! It'll be so good to see the kids!" Stephanie hugged her. "Val, you are still coming back here to live, aren't you?"

Valerie's hesitation was imperceptible. "Yes, I'm coming back," she said.

She didn't even wait to say goodbye. C. C. Wyatt replaced the telephone receiver with telling precision. When his secretary had given him Valerie's message, he had immediately called the nursery, only to learn that she'd already left.

"Well, let her go, then," he muttered, his pride rebelling against the hurt clawing at his heart. It was better this way, he thought, without defining what *it* was. At any rate, the clean, hot anger flooding his veins was a balm to a badly scratched male ego. He'd tried his best, hadn't he?

But as day followed cheerless day, his anger burned out, leaving behind only an icy knot of loneliness to buffer his pride. He hated coming home to a dark, empty house, anyway, and stayed late at the office most evenings. But eventually even his work wasn't strong enough to block his disorderly tangle of thoughts.

One rainy afternoon, faced with the prospect of another joyless weekend, C.C. left work early and returned home, defeated by the grayness both inside and out. Putting his mail and newspapers down on the kitchen desk, he squinted at the calendar. Yep, he thought ironically, it's still just ten days since she left. It felt like a year.

According to Stephanie, she meant to come back. To him? That was the question that punched him in the stomach each time he thought about it. So many of his thoughts packed a punch these days that he would shy away from thinking entirely if he could. But he couldn't. Valerie was a bright, shining presence in his mind, and nothing, not even logic, could diminish her lovely image.

Sighing, he fixed himself a cup of instant coffee and moodily drank half of it before realizing that what he really wanted was a stiff drink.

But even his finest whiskey didn't help what ailed him. He took a huge swallow and felt the twelve-year-old Scotch burn all the way to his toes. Yet its considerable heat didn't touch the chill deep inside him.

He missed her, missed her with an ache that made her last absence seem like a pinch on the arm. He was sorely tempted to just go to Mississippi and get her. But that might be the wrong thing to do.

Another heavy sigh stirred his mustache. He'd done everything else wrong, he couldn't afford to mess up again. There were so many things he should have done differently. He should have claimed her for his own the first time he'd kissed her and felt the kind of sparkling, joyous passion he'd thought never to feel again. But he'd hemmed and hawed, trying to protect himself against the risk of getting hurt. By life, not just her, although God knew she was a vital part of his life. The misery of these past days and nights without her had shown him that.

And he should have made love to her the moment she'd told him about her terrible ordeal, he berated himself. But thinking he knew exactly what was right for her, he had gone the opposite route, being kind and compassionate as hell, when he should have just picked her up and borne her off to his bed.

And he sure shouldn't have turned on that damned light. And after the fact, he should have been more forceful, should have held her there until he'd had his say.

I should have told her I loved her. C.C. rubbed his scratchy eyelids. He still wasn't sure about that. Oh, not about loving her—that was gritty reality—but about telling her. Once he did, then what? He rubbed his eyes again. Ultimately he would have to deal with the chance of losing someone else that he loved. *Was loving again worth the risk of such terrible pain?*

Evading that question for the moment, he went on to the next one. Would telling her have done any good? In hindsight, he doubted it. She was so outraged by his stupidity. Well, all right, he had been stupid. But a man could learn, couldn't he? A man could stop being so afraid of love that he'd deny it even when it was hitting him in the face.

It was time to make a move. With a brash determination, C.C. put on his Stetson and dialed the airport. A moment later the only things moving in the big white kitchen were the swinging doors.

It was odd to feel like an alien on the streets of her own town, Valerie reflected. But she did. Home just didn't fit anymore. Her concept of the word kept alternating between Stephanie's house and C.C.'s.

Feeling her irritation increase, she shook her head as if to dislodge any thoughts of C.C. She'd forgotten to stop at the market for milk. Well, they could just do without. Along with throbbing temples, she felt stuffed up from her nose to her forehead, which wasn't surprising. Since her crying jag, she hadn't wept again despite a rather desperate need to do so now and then. I probably have a whole lake of tears dammed up behind my eyelids, she thought sourly.

Her heart ached incessantly, but she hadn't been wallowing in despair during her ten days home. She'd already gotten estimates from two moving companies, arranged for her lawyer to handle the sale of her husband's business and even managed to get most of her Christmas shopping done before Nana and the children arrived yesterday afternoon. They had trimmed the tree last night and enjoyed a tea party afterward. Merry little faces and giggling laughter had filled the big living room.

Determined to provide her children with a happy Christmas, Valerie had concealed her sadness behind a smile. Unlike Stephanie, painful acceptance had been very much a part of her own life, and she was good at hiding her true emotions. No use upsetting others just because you're in a blue funk, she thought with a philosophical shrug.

During this week she had also consulted her surgeon and made an appointment with her family doctor for a complete checkup the first week of January.

Just routine, Valerie assured herself. She knew what he would say: excellent chance for total recovery with no recurrence. He had to say that. If he didn't...a stern shake of head rejected that possibility. She would not dwell on thoughts of a negative prognosis. That way lay madness. But neither could she forget that the possibility did, always, exist.

Another reason to make a clean break with C.C., she thought, proceeding through the light. He'd already lost one mate.

But how she would deal with C.C.'s constant nearness when she returned to Texas was an agonizing question. After less than two weeks' absence, her need for him was a physical ache. But somehow they would have to regress back to friends again.

Grimacing at the stab of pain engendered by that thought, she turned onto a street partially paved with old red bricks that led to her home. A woman waved at her and Valerie waved back. Clinton was a typically friendly little Southern town, and Nana, having lived there most of her married life, knew practically everyone in it, which meant that practically everyone knew Valerie.

It was a family-oriented neighborhood, with children racing through the big yards enjoying the last rays of a spectacular sunset. Homes were aglow with Christmas lights and ornaments. Her own was warm and inviting with golden lamplight and the gaily lit tree shining through the big bay window.

Her heart lifted as she thought of Stephanie's arrival day after tomorrow. Valerie was surprised at how much she missed her sister's warm and lovely presence. That was one solid reason never to regret her Texas visit, she thought softly.

Nana's car was gone from the carport. She and the children were going to the mall to do their own shopping and evidently had already left.

Valerie gave the strange car parked in front of the house no more than a desultory glance. Neighboring visitors often parked on the street, Gathering her gloves and briefcase, she walked into the house.

She sensed someone's presence even before she reached the living room. C. C. Wyatt was sitting in a green velvet wing chair turning his Stetson around and around in his big hands.

She caught her breath and slowly released it, cleared her throat and tested her voice. "C.C."

Placing his hat on the table, C.C. stood. "Hello, Valerie. I missed you," he said, getting directly to the point.

Valerie tried to move and succeeded only in shifting her stance. "Hello... How did you get in here?" she blurted.

He stepped closer. "Elizabeth let me in."

"You met my mother-in-law? And she just let you come in and wait?"

The corners of his mouth lifted. "Yes. In fact, we hit it off. I liked her and she liked me. An intelligent woman."

"Oh. And my children?" Valerie's heart, already pounding, gave an alarming jump. "Did you meet them?"

"Yes, I met them."

Valerie was helpless to stem the rush of eagerness affecting her voice as she asked, "What did you think of my girls?"

"They're lovely, of course. A rare combination of you and their own special selves. They asked if I was your boyfriend and I said certainly I was."

"I see," Valerie said faintly. "And what did they say?"

He grinned. "They thought I was neat-o. Of course I agreed with them. You're a lucky woman, Valerie, to have such fine children."

"Thank you," Valerie said, slanting him a glance. Naturally he'd find my weakness right off, she thought wryly. "What are you doing here, C.C.? You're the last person I expected to find in my living room."

"When you left Texas, you left behind some unfinished business."

Breaking through the paralysis of surprise and elation, she shrugged off her jacket and tossed it on the couch. "What unfinished business?"

"Me."

He stepped closer, until she could smell his clean familiar scent. He needed a haircut. And she needed to lose both her hands in that tawny, shaggy thatch.

"C.C." She shook her head. "I don't understand."

"It's very simple. I told myself I didn't care that you'd left without even a goodbye. I lied. I cared, all right. I should have told you so, that last night. But I was angry, too angry to try calling you later. First because you'd left without caring how I felt and that hurt. Second, because I felt belittled, having you think I wouldn't want you because you're less than perfect.''

He slid a hand to her cheek in a heart-stilling caress. "I readily admit I wasn't very smart, Val. I did everything wrong. From start to finish, I was wrong. I should have told you earlier how much you mattered to me. And I was surely wrong to turn that light on, to catch you so badly unprepared. I did it because I was afraid you were using your mastectomy to build a wall between us. But that doesn't excuse it.''

"No, it doesn't," she quietly agreed.

C.C. sighed and ran a hand through his rumpled hair. "And after it happened, I should have spoken out, made you listen to me, told you how lovely and desirable you are and how I wanted you as passionately as ever, and that I'd go crazy if you ever left me." His mustache quirked. "I guess the reason I didn't tell you the last part of that was because I didn't know until you had left.''

"Oh, C.C.," she said softly. "I didn't leave just because I wanted to shock you into realizing you'd miss me. I left because I love you, and I didn't want to force you into anything. You're an honorable man and you might have felt...responsible pity or something.''

"Hogwash. What I felt was anything *but* responsible pity." His head jerked up. "You love me? Well, why the hell didn't you say so!" he exploded joyously.

"There didn't seem to be a proper time for it," she murmured. "Besides, I didn't know if it was returned. Come to think of it, I still don't know. Do you love me, C. C. Wyatt?" she asked with a smile beginning to curve her mouth. She could see the answer in his beautiful eyes.

"Lord, yes, I do! Oh, come here, woman," he growled. Sweeping her into his crushing embrace, C.C. kissed her with all the love and need and desire flaming through his soul.

Valerie's fingers curled into his hair as she returned his kiss with matching ardor. They clung to each other for a long, sensuous moment of togetherness.

"What did you feel when you looked at me that night," she asked softly.

"All mixed up. Shocked, furious, outraged, and a curious sensation of my bones turning to water because I felt so damn much love and tenderness and compassion," he returned gruffly. "So." He blew out his breath. "Why were you so quick to judge me, to think I wouldn't want you after I'd seen you?"

She tucked her face into the curve of his neck and shoulder. "There were several reasons. You know about that bad experience I had with another man. That influenced me more than I realized, I guess. And I suppose I hadn't quite come to terms with my altered self-image. Oh, C.C., I do love you." She pressed against his long body, arching her back into his caressing hands. The taste and touch and scent of him filled a vital need and she wanted never to let him go. But she had to.

Rubbing her cheek against his, she said, "I really do love you. That's another reason why I thought it might be best to break it off. Because you've already gone through the grief and trauma of losing one beloved woman, and with me, well, there are no guarantees, C.C."

Indignation tinged C.C.'s voice. "Valerie, I hear what you're saying, but what do you think I am, a fairweather lover? If the situation was reversed, would you walk out on me? Besides, I don't come with a guarantee, either, babe. Who does? But together we make a strong team, honey. My strength is here for you when you falter, and vice versa. End of discussion."

"No, not quite," she said, pulling back from him. "I've consulted a surgeon, C.C. He says it's possible to reconstruct my breast, and I've decided to do it."

"Valerie, that isn't necessary, not for me, it isn't," C.C. protested.

"No, I'm doing this for myself, darling. It isn't a decision I made lightly—I'm scared to death! But I want to feel like a complete woman again."

"I'll support whatever you decide, just as long as you know how I feel. To me, you're perfect just the way you are, Val. In fact," he growled, "I'm aching to get my hands on all that perfection!"

He kissed her O-shaped lips. "Now. I love you very much, Valerie Audra Hepburn. Will you marry me and be my wife?"

She laughed and flung her arms around his neck. "Being your wife will certainly be a marvelous way to spend the rest of my life, C. C. Wyatt! But don't let's rush it, love, let's take it wonderfully slow and easy. I'm a sucker for a tender, romantic, madly passionate courtship," she confided.

"You are, hmm?" C.C. wrapped her in his arms again, marveling at her delicacy, loving the sweet, essential perfume exuded by her soft skin. "So am I, now that I've met you. Are you free for some of that, ah, togetherness tonight?" he asked huskily.

Valerie gave him a stern look. "C.C., really! It is almost Christmas and my family will be back any minute. We can wait. After all," she murmured against his fine mouth, "we have all the time in the world."

*   *   *   *   *

This is the season of giving, and Silhouette proudly offers you its sixth annual Christmas collection.

SILHOUETTE

Christmas Stories

1991

Experience the joys of a holiday romance and treasure these heart-warming stories by four award-winning Silhouette authors:

Phyllis Halldorson—"A Memorable Noel"
Peggy Webb—"I Heard the Rabbits Singing"
Naomi Horton—"Dreaming of Angels"
Heather Graham Pozzessere—"The Christmas Bride"

Discover this yuletide celebration—sit back and enjoy Silhouette's Christmas gift of love.

SILHOUETTE®
OFFICIAL SWEEPSTAKES
RULES

NO PURCHASE NECESSARY

1. To enter, complete an Official Entry Form or 3" × 5" index card by hand-printing, in plain block letters, your complete name, address, phone number and age, and mailing it to: Silhouette Fashion A Whole New You Sweepstakes, P.O. Box 9056, Buffalo, NY 14269-9056.

   No responsibility is assumed for lost, late or misdirected mail. Entries must be sent separately with first class postage affixed, and be received no later than December 31, 1991 for eligibility.

2. Winners will be selected by D.L. Blair, Inc., an independent judging organization whose decisions are final, in random drawings to be held on January 30, 1992 in Blair, NE at 10:00 a.m. from among all eligible entries received.

3. The prizes to be awarded and their approximate retail values are as follows: Grand Prize — A brand-new Ford Explorer 4×4 plus a trip for two (2) to Hawaii, including round-trip air transportation, six (6) nights hotel accommodation, a $1,400 meal/spending money stipend and $2,000 cash toward a new fashion wardrobe (approximate value: $28,000) or $15,000 cash; two (2) Second Prizes — A trip to Hawaii, including round-trip air transportation, six (6) nights hotel accommodation, a $1,400 meal/spending money stipend and $2,000 cash toward a new fashion wardrobe (approximate value: $11,000) or $5,000 cash; three (3) Third Prizes — $2,000 cash toward a new fashion wardrobe. All prizes are valued in U.S. currency. Travel award air transportation is from the commercial airport nearest winner's home. Travel is subject to space and accommodation availability, and must be completed by June 30, 1993. Sweepstakes offer is open to residents of the U.S. and Canada who are 21 years of age or older as of December 31, 1991, except residents of Puerto Rico, employees and immediate family members of Torstar Corp., its affiliates, subsidiaries, and all agencies, entities and persons connected with the use, marketing, or conduct of this sweepstakes. All federal, state, provincial, municipal and local laws apply. Offer void wherever prohibited by law. Taxes and/or duties, applicable registration and licensing fees, are the sole responsibility of the winners. Any litigation within the province of Quebec respecting the conduct and awarding of a prize may be submitted to the Régie des loteries et courses du Québec. All prizes will be awarded; winners will be notified by mail. No substitution of prizes is permitted.

4. Potential winners must sign and return any required Affidavit of Eligibility/Release of Liability within 30 days of notification. In the event of noncompliance within this time period, the prize may be awarded to an alternate winner. Any prize or prize notification returned as undeliverable may result in the awarding of that prize to an alternate winner. By acceptance of their prize, winners consent to use of their names, photographs or their likenesses for purposes of advertising, trade and promotion on behalf of Torstar Corp. without further compensation. Canadian winners must correctly answer a time-limited arithmetical question in order to be awarded a prize.

5. For a list of winners (available after 3/31/92), send a separate stamped, self-addressed envelope to: Silhouette Fashion A Whole New You Sweepstakes, P.O. Box 4665, Blair, NE 68009.

PREMIUM OFFER TERMS

To receive your gift, complete the Offer Certificate according to directions. Be certain to enclose the required number of "Fashion A Whole New You" proofs of product purchase (which are found on the last page of every specially marked "Fashion A Whole New You" Silhouette or Harlequin romance novel). Requests must be received no later than December 31, 1991. Limit: four (4) gifts per name, family, group, organization or address. Items depicted are for illustrative purposes only and may not be exactly as shown. Please allow 6 to 8 weeks for receipt of order. Offer good while quantities of gifts last. In the event an ordered gift is no longer available, you will receive a free, previously unpublished Silhouette or Harlequin book for every proof of purchase you have submitted with your request, plus a refund of the postage and handling charge you have included. Offer good in the U.S. and Canada only.

SLFW-SWPR

SILHOUETTE® OFFICIAL SWEEPSTAKES ENTRY FORM

4-FWSDS-4

Complete and return this Entry Form immediately – the more entries you submit, the better your chances of winning!

- Entries must be received by **December 31, 1991.**
- A Random draw will take place on **January 30, 1992.**
- No purchase necessary.

Yes, I want to win a FASHION A WHOLE NEW YOU Sensuous and Adventurous prize from Silhouette:

Name _____ Telephone _____ Age _____

Address _____

City _____ State _____ Zip _____

Return Entries to: **Silhouette FASHION A WHOLE NEW YOU,**
P.O. Box 9056, Buffalo, NY 14269-9056   © 1991 Harlequin Enterprises Limited

PREMIUM OFFER

To receive your free gift, send us the required number of proofs-of-purchase from any specially marked FASHION A WHOLE NEW YOU Silhouette or Harlequin Book with the Offer Certificate properly completed, plus a check or money order (do not send cash) to cover postage and handling payable to Silhouette FASHION A WHOLE NEW YOU Offer. We will send you the specified gift.

OFFER CERTIFICATE

Item	A. SENSUAL DESIGNER VANITY BOX COLLECTION (set of 4) (Suggested Retail Price $60.00)	B. ADVENTUROUS TRAVEL COSMETIC CASE SET (set of 3) (Suggested Retail Price $25.00)
# of proofs-of-purchase	18	12
Postage and Handling	$3.50	$2.95
Check one	☐	☐

Name _____

Address _____

City _____ State _____ Zip _____

Mail this certificate, designated number of proofs-of-purchase and check or money order for postage and handling to: **Silhouette FASHION A WHOLE NEW YOU Gift Offer,** P.O. Box 9057, Buffalo, NY 14269-9057. Requests must be received by December 31, 1991.

ONE PROOF-OF-PURCHASE

4-FWSDP-4

To collect your fabulous free gift you must include the necessary number of proofs-of-purchase with a properly completed Offer Certificate.

© 1991 Harlequin Enterprises Limited

See previous page for details.